A
Fabulous
Creature

OTHER YEARLING BOOKS YOU WILL ENJOY:

Zilpha Keatley
Snyder

*A
Fabulous
Creature*

A YEARLING BOOK

Published by
Dell Publishing
a division of
The Bantam Doubleday Dell Publishing Group, Inc.
666 Fifth Avenue
New York, New York 10103

ISBN: 0-440-40179-8

Reprinted by arrangement with Macmillan Publishing Co., Inc.,
on behalf of Atheneum Publishers

Printed in the United States of America

December 1988

10 9 8 7 6 5 4 3 2 1

CW

To Larry

A Fabulous Creature

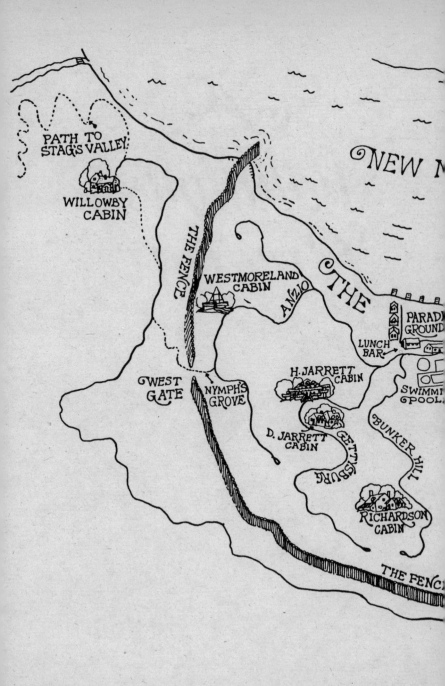

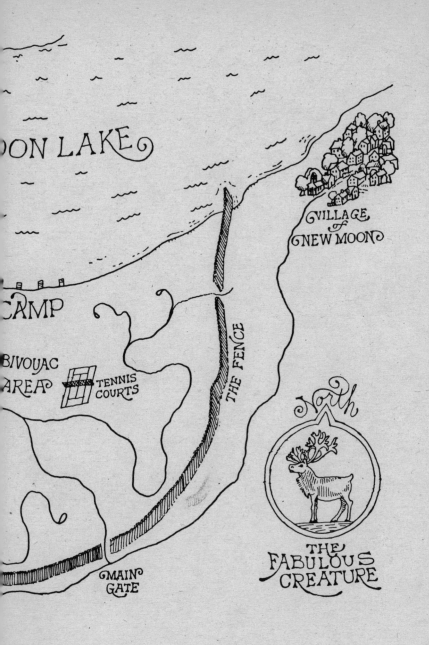

DON LAKE

VILLAGE
of
NEW MOON

CAMP

BIVOUAC
AREA

TENNIS
COURTS

THE FENCE

North

MAIN
GATE

THE
FABULOUS
CREATURE

CHAPTER 1

THE DEER turned quickly and froze, its sleek, wild head balancing the massive crown of horns with amazing ease. Except for its wide ears, scanning like radar saucers, it had become a living statue.

Only a few yards away, crouched on the flat surface of a large boulder, James Fielding held his breath and tried to quiet the thunder of his heart. But the deer had heard, or perhaps sensed, something because it began to move cautiously away. With taut, delicate precision, it edged toward the trees, its muscles bunched and triggered for instant flight. But then, quite suddenly, it stopped and tested the air with quivering nostrils. For several seconds it read and reread the message carried by the moist air, and then—to James' wild excitement—it came slowly towards him. When it reached the spot where he had left the apples, it stopped to look directly at him before it lowered its head. It was so near now that he clearly heard the juicy crunch as it accepted his offering. When the apples were gone, it once more returned his gaze before it began to move away. At the edge of the clearing it seemed to blur and then to melt with magical suddenness into the gray-green underbrush that edged the clearing.

He flipped over on his back and let out a long sigh of relaxed tension. For a few seconds he lay staring up toward white clouds and the blue clarity of mountain air, but seeing only the swift, wild turn of the horned head. Purposely shutting out his mind, he floated on a high, serene excitement, knowing that it would disappear if he tried to analyze it. At last he sighed again, grinned, and blinked his eyes rapidly. Taking off his glasses, he wiped them on his tee shirt and hooked them back over his ears.

"The noble stag," he said out loud. And a moment later, "The stag at eve had drunk its fill—where danced the moon on—on . . ." He'd forgotten what came next. He sat up, looked at his watch, and lunged to his feet. Partway across the boulder, moving with his usual cat-like agility—James Fielding, expert mountaineer—he managed to slip on a patch of moss and kept himself from pitching over the edge only by a windmill-like maneuver of his long arms and legs. Typical. But fortunately no one was watching, except a couple of astonished chipmunks.

His balance finally regained, he slid down the rest of the way and started off toward the steep, slippery slope that led up to the only entrance to the box canyon. He was still grinning as he started the climb—at himself and the startled chipmunks, but also because it had been a good day. One of the best since the Fieldings had given up civilization for the wilds of the Sierra Nevada Mountains.

When Professor William J. Fielding and his wife, collaborator, personal secretary and general manager, whose name was Charlotte, had arranged to rent a colleague's cabin in the Sierras for the summer, they hadn't consulted James Archer Fielding, their only son and heir, because they were so certain that he would be delighted. They had decided, they said, to surprise him. Instead, he had surprised them by being politely but unshakably opposed to the whole project. Charlotte and William had been mystified and bewildered. Everything they'd ever read—and over the years they'd done a considerable amount of research on the subject—had led them to believe that a fifteen-year-old boy would be wild with joy at the prospect of spending three months in the wilderness on the shore of a beautiful mountain lake. But then, it wasn't as if it was the first time they'd been surprised, not to mention mystified and bewildered. In spite of having come late and rather absentmindedly to parenthood and having, by chance, produced an offspring who had, almost from birth, refused to fit into any of the behavior patterns approved by the proper authorities, the Fieldings had begun parenting with good intentions and at least a fair amount of enthusiasm. But confusion had set in almost immediately.

There had been no reference materials that explained how to approach an infant who composed poetry before he was fully house-trained, and who, after taking a few bad falls, decided walking wasn't worth the risk and put off further efforts until he was eighteen months old and able to justify his preference for crawling in fairly complete sentences.

In the years that followed, William and Charlotte

had largely given up on scientific childrearing and had drifted into the habit of treating James as an undersized and unpredictable colleague who had unaccountably become a semi-permanent guest—a state of affairs of which James highly approved. But every now and then an old-fashioned happy-boyhood theory cropped up—usually with disastrous results—such as: a summer in the wilderness.

Actually a large part of their problem had been timing. Any other summer James might have accepted the proposal without undue protest. Not enthusiastically, perhaps, but with his usual tolerance for such well-intentioned blunders. But it just so happened that this particular summer he and Max had been planning something very different. Something so important that it just might have changed the entire future course of his existence. But the wilderness had won out. And, as it turned out, it wasn't even really wilderness. Not any more. All along the south shore of New Moon Lake there was now —The Camp.

Having reached the narrow trail that skirted the cliff face above Peter's Creek, James was on a high ledge from which the central buildings of The Camp were clearly visible across the lake. "The Camp," as he had written to Max, "is over fifty acres of prime forest and lake front that was sold a few years ago to a developer who proceeded to build about thirty homes—referred to in The Camp's full color brochure as *cabins* or *quarters*. You know what a *cabin* is, don't you, Max? You can tell it's a cabin if it has rustic hand-tooled leather furniture, a sunken tub in only one of its four bathrooms and only a very small wet bar. Then, after surrounding the whole

6

complex with chain link and barbed wire—no land mines yet but they're probably on order—they found appropriate buyers, the kind with enormous bank accounts and even bigger anxiety complexes. I think most of the owners are planning to hole up here *come the revolution*, but in the meantime it gives them a place to sop it up while pretending to live a rugged *frontier-fort* type of existence." It had been one of his better letters. Max had liked it a lot.

Standing now at the highest point of the trail, James could see the sharply pitched roofs of The Camp's community center and indoor swimming pool, and a few of the boathouses. Just beyond lay the gym with its saunas and hot tubs and the open pavillion where the dances—cleverly referred to in The Camp Bulletin as "Close-Order-Drills"—were held. And beyond that the park area where the whole community gathered for Sunday Bivouacs—catered picnics, actually, but very strenuous and rugged with all *troops* lining up for *mess*, served in authentic U.S. Army tin plates, which Major T. J. Mitchell, the camp manager, had had to pull all kinds of strings to acquire—let me tell you. In fact, a whole page in a recent Bulletin had been devoted to an appreciation of T.J.'s string-pulling—tinplatewise. It had been, James was sure, a high point in the history of bulletin publishing. He'd have to remember to send a copy to Max.

Of course, the old Willowby cabin, in which the Fieldings were spending the summer, was on the outside, well beyond The Camp's barbed wire fortifications. But the Fieldings had been granted access. As a rule, outsiders, without a specific invitation, were turned back at the gatehouse, where an armed guard—*sentry* in T.J.ese

7

—was on twenty-four-hour duty. However, a special dispensation had been made for Willowby guests and renters. Major Mitchell had issued a special pass that allowed Willowbyites to enter in order to shop at the Commissary. It was, after all, only fair since the huge complex had wiped out the old road, which had once led from the Willowby property to the village of New Moon and the only other grocery store in fifteen miles.

So James had been on the sacred soil many times on shopping trips for his mother. He didn't mind going, actually. He considered The Camp an interesting social phenomenon—and Max thought it was an absolute riot. Max had written that he had laughed himself into stomach spasms over James' last letter on the subject.

After the steep and tricky descent to the Peter's Creek crossing, a shallow stretch of water sprinkled with stepping stones, the trail followed the southern bank and then plunged down a long decline to the lake shore. A hundred yards along the shore the trail turned to the right and began a short, steep ascent to the cabin. To the left lay the Willowby section of lake front. Sandy and rock free, it was one of the nicest beaches on New Moon Lake. When James reached the shore, the sun had just gone behind the jagged ridge of Six Prong Mountain, but the smooth sand was still cosily warm to the touch. He glanced at his watch and then, tired from the long climb across the cliff face, sank down to rest before taking on the last lap to home and dinner. Within moments he was half asleep.

When the golf ball missed his nose by a scant inch and thudded into the sand beyond his head, he sat up with a start, thinking for a moment that he had been shot at. Then, on seeing the ball, he wondered rather irrationally if it had come all the way from The Camp putting green. It didn't seem likely, but where else could it have come from? Turning to look toward the wooded headland that separated the Willowby beach from The Camp shoreline, he found himself face to face with the answer to his question.

Perhaps it was because he was slightly disoriented, having been startled out of a semi-doze, or perhaps it had something to do with the expression on the golf ball launcher's face—but it took him a moment to realize that what he was staring at was a very young child. But once he'd managed to get past the frown—an arrangement of features that seemed to express a startlingly mature and well-developed degree of hostility—he began to notice certain clues: overall size, roundish shape, and in particular, the soggy cotton training pants that were its only article of apparel. Below the pants were two sturdy legs and above a rather pronounced stomach, a round head and, in the middle of a fat-cheeked face, a nose so buttonlike that he found himself wondering if a quick push at that point might cause a change of expression. Any change at all would have to be for the better.

Still glaring, the kid began to stomp around his erstwhile target in a wide circle. While other persons in its age range might be said to toddle, in this case stomp was definitely the more accurate verb. It was on its way to retrieve its missile and then, undoubtedly, would attack again. James was gathering himself for an attempt at interception, when someone shouted from the direction of the lake.

"Jacky. You come here this minute."

The new arrival was bikini-clad, probably mid-teens and unmistakably female. A girl, in fact, whom James had specifically noticed twice before during visits to The Camp. The first time talking to a goggle-eyed young man in front of the Commissary, and a few days later on the tennis courts wearing a very short white dress. He remembered particularly because on each occasion, several of Max's favorite comments had run through his mind. The female sex was one of a great many subjects on which Max was an authority, and there were several things about this girl's appearance that he would certainly have mentioned. But at the moment even Max's best comments seemed inadequate—or would have if James had been able to remember any of them.

Wading towards the shore, a pink and tan goddess, risen wet and glistening from the dark waters of the lake, the girl was—terrifying. With a sinking sensation James recognized familiar symptoms: a withering tongue and a brain turning to frozen mush. In total violation of the first Maxian Law—STAY COOL—he succumbed to consternation as the hot-pink-bikinied apparition stopped a few feet away, tipped her head to one side, scooped scattered strands of wet blonde hair into a coil and began slowly to wring them out, all the while regarding James with a thoughtful frown.

He tried to return the frown, tried to smile, tried desperately to pretend he'd never noticed her in the first place, and wound up croaking a witless, "Hi." It was obvious, however, that only his speaking voice had been stricken, because simultaneously his interior voice was clearly telling him what an ass he was making of himself. The girl went on wringing and frowning.

After several eternities her eyes narrowed, and biting her lip, she aimed a finger, pistol-fashion, at his chest. "Ka-pow!" she said, cocking her thumb. "Got it."

"Got wh-what?"

"I got it. Where I've seen you before. Weren't you hanging around the tennis courts the other day?"

Encouraged by the thought that he'd been noticed —possibly favorably?—he regained the use of at least a part of his wits. "Yes," he said with what he hoped was quiet dignity, "I was at the courts a few days ago."

Abruptly the girl stopped wringing out her hair, and sitting down, she pulled one of her feet up into her lap and began to examine its sandy pink bottom. "I know," she said. "I noticed you. The glasses and . . ." She glanced at him appraisingly, ". . . and everything. I stepped on something sharp in that crummy lake."

James, who could function perfectly well without his glasses except when he wanted to see things very distinctly at a great distance, resisted the urge to snatch them off. "I noticed you, too," he began lamely—and then was suddenly stricken by a truly Maxian inspiration. He was just gathering his wits to comment suavely on how particularly he'd noticed her, and perhaps even on how very noticeable she was in general, when he was stricken even more forcibly—just below the left shoulder blade. "Ow!" he yelled, leaping to his feet and whirling around in an awkward, sand-scattering convulsion.

Completely ignoring his victim, the infant hit-man was chugging through the sand in the direction taken by his self-propelled dumdum. Still in considerable pain, James shocked himself by almost succumbing to an urge to kick the kid's feet out from under him before he reached his objective. However, the golf ball, after ricocheting off James' shoulder blade, had rolled in the direction of the girl, and now she quickly retrieved it by uncoiling herself and stretching backward in a startlingly graceful and sinuous movement.

Bellowing indignantly, the infant charged her, but she dexterously stiff-armed him and then, with one hand on his fat middle, calmly held him at arm's length while he continued to roar and strike at her hand and arm with small fat-padded fists.

"Isn't he gross?" she said, smiling with surprising tolerance at the kid who was now trying to bite off one of her fingers.

For some reason the little monster helped. James found that he was relaxing. Probably because with all that yelling and slugging and biting going on, it was impossible for even the most confirmed paranoid to go on considering himself to be the center of possibly unfavorable attention. So he could allow a shred of normal curiosity to enter his brain. It suddenly occurred to him to wonder how the kid had gotten from The Camp to the Willowby beach, since the famous fence separated the beaches, extending well out into the deep water of the lake.

"Where did he come from, anyway?" he asked, glancing toward the top of the fence, just visible beyond the headland.

The girl giggled. "Where do you suppose he came from?" she said, rolling her eyes suggestively.

James felt his face beginning to get hot and, no doubt, red—a ridiculous physical characteristic that had always played a part in his lack of social assurance. "I mean . . ." He pointed limply towards the fence. "How did—"

"My mother got careless, I guess." With practiced skill she traded arms, shoving the kid backwards and catching him again with her other hand as he charged forward. "Can you imagine anything so gross. After I'd had thirteen years to get used to being the youngest, she has to go and have this monster."

He actually relaxed enough to laugh. "What I meant was—" he began, but she interrupted again.

"Wait a minute. He's wearing me out. I've got to get rid of him for a minute." Holding out the golf ball she said, "Look Jacky. Here it is. Here's your ball. Now, go get it." She threw the ball as hard as she could down the beach.

Jacky gave a final angry yelp and trotted off, while the girl watched him go approvingly. "He's a real killer," she said. "Isn't he? I mean for barely two years old?"

Wrapping one of his arms around his neck, James gingerly explored his shoulder blade with the tips of his fingers. "You can say that again," he said grimly.

She glanced at him quickly, as if surprised. "Oh, the golf ball." She shrugged. "Well, don't take it personally. He throws it at everyone."

"Yeah? Why do you let him? I mean, why doesn't someone just take it away from him?"

"Oh, we couldn't do that. He has to have it. It's a psychological thing. My mom did take it away once, when our cook quit because he hit her in the souffle, but it didn't do any good. All he did was scream the house down until he got it back. Even when he just loses it— look out!" Making pistols of both her hands she shot them off into her temples. "Ka-pow! He drives everyone crazy until he gets it back. Besides my dad doesn't want us to take it away. He thinks Jacky's old golf ball is a real riot."

"Doesn't he ever throw it at him? At your dad?"

"Oh sure. He doesn't mind."

James shrugged. "Look," he said. "What I was trying to ask was, how he got out of The Camp?"

"Oh, that. He crawled under. Down there where the fence goes over those flat boulders at the edge of the beach. There's a place where the rock dips down a little, and he squeezed through. He wouldn't come back when I called so I had to swim out around the end of the fence." She sighed. "I've been stuck with him all afternoon. My mom is in the tennis tournament. I probably should have just let him get lost or whatever, except then I wouldn't have gotten my twenty dollars."

"Twenty dollars? Just for baby-sitting?"

"Sure. For a whole afternoon with Jacky? What it's really worth is more like a thousand."

Glancing up, James noticed Jacky stomping purposefully in their direction, golf ball clutched in sandy fist. "Well, now that you mention it . . ." he said. The girl was crouching slightly preparing to dodge, and he followed her example.

"Look out," she said. "Here it comes." The ball whistled between them, and running after it, she scooped it up and headed towards the fence. "I've got to go," she called. "Come over here and help me get him through the fence."

James followed, wondering how she planned to get Jacky through the hole, which looked as if it would be a tight squeeze, if he didn't want to go. Would she try to stuff him through it, or—he grinned, contemplating a more satisfying possibility—perhaps, throw him over the top? But when he reached the fence the problem had already been partly solved. The girl had thrown the golf ball through the fence, and Jacky was already frantically burrowing after it. Now all that remained for James to do was to make sure he didn't come back while his sister was swimming around the end of the barricade.

It wasn't too difficult. When Jacky tried to crawl back under, James sat down and, instead of vulnerable hands, used a toothproof hiking boot to shove him back to the other side. And when the kid gave up on the hole and threatened to golf ball him through the fence, he simply spoke to him firmly. "You throw that thing over here, you little turkey, and you'll never see it again." He wasn't sure how much of that Jacky understood, but it seemed to be enough. He was still clutching his Spaulding torpedo when his sister rose from the lake like a hot pink mermaid. Grabbing his wrist she towed him, stiff-legged and bellowing, toward the center of The Camp.

James was still peering through the fence, watching them go with very mixed feelings, when she stopped suddenly and looked back. "Hey!" she called. "I'm Diane Jarrett. Who are you?"

"James! James Fielding!" he shouted, and for once his voice didn't crack at the crucial moment. In fact, it burst forth with surprising resonance. Like the trumpeting of a bull moose in mating season—he would tell Max. Max would crack up.

CHAPTER 2

I SAID, 'How is Leonardo?' As a matter of fact, it's the third time I've said, 'How is Leonardo?' Where are you this morning, James?"

"What? Oh, I'm sorry." James brought himself back to bacon and eggs and his mother's anxious frown from across the breakfast table. "Leonardo is fine. I just have the Jenkins book to finish reading, and I'll be ready to start the actual writing."

"Well," Charlotte said, "I should think you'd have to start soon if you're going to be able to get it in the mail to Mr. Johnson by August."

Charlotte meant well, but she was just too accustomed to coping with a husband who made your average run-of-the-mill absentminded professor look like an efficiency expert. James' father did several things extremely well. He was an excellent lecturer, writer, and historical researcher and a real genius at infecting other people with his own passionate interest in history. But he was a total failure at certain aspects of daily life. At the university Professor Fielding was famous for his tendency to misplace such things as his glasses, his lunch, his wallet, his lecture notes, and, on an average of once a week, his 1969 Volvo. Even after Charlotte had it painted bright red. Half the people on campus had a funny story about helping him rummage through all six of the campus parking lots looking for it. There were a lot of other stories, too. One of the most famous dated back to the pre-Volvo days when Professor Fielding used to walk to school in good weather. One morning Charlotte had handed him the garbage pail to deposit on the curb as he left, and some time later he had arrived in the classroom with his briefcase in one hand and the garbage in the other. In fact, James sometimes privately compared his father to a very powerful airplane that had somehow been manufactured without a starter, navigational device, or a steering mechanism. Over the years there would have been a lot of crashes if it hadn't been for Charlotte.

James, himself, on the other hand, was an entirely different matter. Very early on—perhaps as a reaction to hearing his father chuckled about—he had decided to be famous someday, not only for his creative genius—exact area yet to be decided upon—but also for his brisk efficiency in everyday matters.

"Don't worry," he told his mother. "The essay will be done in plenty of time." The essay on Leonardo da Vinci was the extra credit project that James had contracted to do as a part of his petition to finish high school in three years instead of four. The research was really no problem, since he had been a da Vinci fan for years—ever since William's sabbatical, which the Fieldings had spent in Italy, near the village where Leonardo was born. There was, however, some reading he'd meant to do. He'd come to the wilderness equipped with a couple of new biographies, which he'd intended to read before he began to write. And, although there was no reason at all for Charlotte to worry, he had to admit that he hadn't accomplished nearly as much as he'd intended to by now. What had made the difference was the fact that the wilderness hadn't turned out to be as much of a bore as he'd expected.

At first it had been the forest itself. Before that summer James hadn't particularly related to trees, having been well acquainted with only the few rather uninspired specimens to be found in backyards and in the scientifically groomed and landscaped groves of the university campus. Not that he had anything against them. It was just that trees, as such, had failed to make any significant impact on his philosophy of life in general. But that state of affairs had begun to change almost the moment the Fieldings moved into a cabin entirely surrounded for miles and miles by almost nothing else. The trees were everywhere, ancient stately trees; ragged shaggy undomesticated giants, possessed of towering dignity and a strange, almost intimidating mystery. From the first day he had been strangely and entirely unexpectedly fascinated. Passing up the more obvious pleasures of the lake, the swimming and boating and fishing, he had taken to the woods, spending most of every day exploring deeper and deeper into the surrounding area, much to his parents' mystification. Now and then Charlotte took time out from collaborating with William on his third textbook to worry about it.

"What do you do out there in the woods alone all day?" she would ask, or "Your father and I are planning to take the afternoon off and row out to the island.

Wouldn't you like to come along?" James wouldn't, but he found it difficult to explain why, even to himself.

He had, for a while, considered the possibility that it was a form of regression, that he had suddenly slipped black to his Daniel Boone period. Sifting back through his long history of what Charlotte called hero-worship and William referred to as historical transference, James was able to determine that, if it were true, he must have just lost about seven years. He was sure of the time sequence because he remembered specifically that the Daniel Boone syndrome had followed the Robin Hood phase, both of which had preceeded Julius Ceasar and Alexander the Great, all of which had happened before his tenth birthday—because he definitely recalled that by the time he was ten, he had given up world conquest and decided, instead, to be a universal man. But after further analysis he'd decided that the whole thing had nothing to do with Daniel Boone, or with regression, for that matter. Whatever it was, he was sure it had nothing to do with pretending to be anybody, not even James Archer Fielding.

In fact, when he was alone in the woods, he seemed at times to be scarcely aware of James Archer Fielding at all. What he was aware of was a kind of overwhelming majesty, dignity, and beauty that owed nothing to him or to any other member of the human species. Walking through cathedral groves, dipping his fingers in the pure clarity of natural fonts, climbing high rocky altars, he experienced what seemed to be a kind of spiritual aerobics—as if undeveloped capacities of some mysterious nature were being stretched and challenged. Part of it was a constant feeling of anticipation, of wonders about to be revealed and promises soon to be kept. And then he had stumbled upon the hidden canyon and its magnificent occupant, and it all seemed to come together. The deer became the center of it all, a symbol too secret and significant to be shared or discussed—at least not for the present. To Max he only wrote that nature sometimes does something so perfect that it's almost enough to shake your faith—in agnosticism. And to William and Charlotte he said nothing at all.

At first it had been simple stubbornness. They had said he would love the wilderness, he had said he wouldn't, and he resisted admitting that they'd been right. But before long it was much more than that. Before long it had become the kind of private treasure you don't risk by exposing it to the appraisal of others. Particularly not if the others in question happen to have made a career of investigating other people's value systems in the cold light of logic. There was nothing logical about the way James felt about the deer in the valley—and he didn't want there to be.

"James! You're getting to be as bad as your father." Apparently he'd been daydreaming again and missed something his mother had been saying to him. But now the frustrated shrillness of her voice had gotten through not only to him, but to his father as well.

Looking up from the notebook he'd been scribbling in all through breakfast, William smiled at James. "What's this? What have you been up to to merit such a harsh accusation?"

"Not listening." James grinned. "I stand accused of the heinous sin of not listening."

"Shocking," William said sternly. "Capital offense. Off with his head."

Charlotte smiled, and then sighed with exasperation, at both of them or at herself for smiling at them. "What I've been saying was—we're out of bread and milk again, and I wondered if you'd mind going over to the Commissary for me before you take off for the hills."

For just a moment he felt disappointed—he'd been thinking of taking a lunch and spending the whole day in the valley of the stag; but then suddenly the disappointment faded. Another image had appeared in his mind, taking the place of the noble beast. A hot pink and golden tan image. "Sure," he said. "I'd be glad to."

The west gate of The Camp was a small pedestrian-sized opening, on the opposite side of the enclosure from the main entrance. It was used mostly by Campers on their way into the mountains to hike or ski—and by Willowby-ites on their way to and from the Commissary. There was no gatehouse or guard, but there was a very heavy duty gate. Admission was by remote control. You opened the call box, held down a button, and talked to the guard at the main gate.

"Main gate, Sergeant Smithers speaking. Who goes there?"

James suppressed a laugh. Smithers was the chubby bald guard with the pot belly and slightly embarrassed manner. Embarrassed, no doubt, by having to call himself sergeant when the only army he'd ever been in was probably old T.J.'s, and by having to say corny things like, "Who goes there?"

As far as James had been able to determine, Major

T. J. Mitchell's private army consisted of himself; Lieutenant Carnaby, his fat-legged secretary; old Sergeant Smithers; and the two other gate guards who only got to play they were privates. And then of course, the *troops* —the Camp residents, more than one hundred members of the affluent society ranging in age from doddering to toddling, who seemed, in T.J.'s fantasy, to play the role of a kind of reserve army, but who would be about as effective militarily as a pack of pomeranians, with the possible exception, on second thought, of the little golf ball hit-man.

"James Fielding," he said into the speaker, trying to keep the giggle out of his voice. "Pass number one, eight, five, four, six." The badge number was a case in point— as if The Camp had issued more than eighteen thousand passes. Eight would probably be more like it.

"Okay Fielding. Enter!" Smithers said, and a buzzer sounded, indicating that the gate was unlatched.

Recalling the two-year-old torpedo brought back images—most of which concerned his sister—and the fact that, as far as James was concerned, the main purpose of this expedition was more than the purchase of bread and milk. Man does not live by bread and milk alone. The main purpose was, of course—A. Diane Jarrett. And—B. The Don Juan Project.

The Don Juan Project had begun, or at least the idea had first arisen, in May not too long after James and Max had gotten acquainted. They'd been lying around the swimming pool at the university on one of the afternoons it was reserved for faculty families and their guests, and James had been telling Max, in an amusing and satirical way, about his history of identifying with famous characters from the past. While they were talking, Trudi Hepplewhite, whose father was in chemistry and who was one of the sexiest girls in James' class, came in with three of her friends. It wasn't very long before Max, who didn't know any of the girls, was being suave and cool and just crass enough to be funny and the girls were all cracking up—while James, who had known them for years, was as usual, either saying nothing at all for so long everybody forgot he existed, or else coming up with a boring monologue or some joke that nobody got.

It had been that way with James ever since he'd started taking an interest in girls as such. And that had been a long time ago. Although he seemed to be retarded socially where females were concerned, there was every indication he was normal physically, or even precocious. He'd started thinking seriously about girls fairly early, and the more he thought about them, the more he tied up when they were around. Earlier, much earlier, before sex entered the picture, girls he'd known had been simply people and no particular problem. But the more interested he got, the more he worried about what they were thinking of him and the result was usually—fiasco. Like Heather Rubenstein, for instance. Heather was a neighbor with whom he built tree houses, published a neighborhood paper, started a dog walking business, discussed politics and co-authored several indignant letters to the editor of the *Oakland Tribune*. But then one day he'd noticed some interesting developments where Heather was concerned, and shortly afterwards he'd blown the whole relationship by trying to kiss her. It wasn't that she refused him, either. She'd simply asked him why he wanted to, and he hadn't been able to think of anything to say. And he hadn't been able to think of anything to say to her ever since.

He'd discussed the problem with Max before that day at the pool, but he'd never really leveled with him. It just wasn't easy to admit to someone with Max's experience that you hadn't even kissed a girl—at least not very successfully.

But Max must have guessed. That day at the pool, after the girls had gone, he did something typically Maxian. In the same circumstances anyone else would either have kidded James, or if they were abnormally kindhearted, pretended not to have noticed that he'd made an ass of himself. But Max didn't do either one. What he did do was bring up the subject in a very unemotional way, analyze it, discuss it, and proceed to figure out what could be done about it.

According to Max there wasn't really any reason why James was such a dud where girls were concerned. He was certainly smart, he could be very amusing in the right circumstances, and he wasn't even bad looking.

"Oh sure," James said, flexing his almost nonexistent biceps. "I'm a regular Mr. America."

Max, who not only had a charismatic personality and an attractively homely face, but also a very adequate build, shrugged. "You'll fill out," he said. "I've filled out a lot since I was your age." Max was eleven months older than James. "Besides, there are a lot of women who really go for that unhealthy, soulful look. Look at Peter Frampton and Rod Stewart."

"And Byron and Chopin," James agreed eagerly.

Max regarded him thoughtfully for a minute before he said, "You do have a few problems—but it's nothing that can't be remedied. It's mostly a matter of changing your style and building your confidence." After he'd thought for a while longer he said, "Building your confidence is probably the crucial thing, and I know just the place to do it."

It seemed that the year before, Max had worked for the summer recreation director at St. Mary's, which was a private school for girls. Max had been in charge of keeping the swimming pool area clean and checking out towels and lounge chairs. This year he had moved up to the position of lifeguard and his old job would be open. It was an easy job, and there was plenty of time for socializing. And Max would be there in case James needed advice or moral support. It would be the perfect place for him to get the practice he needed to build his confidence. In fact, Max said he wouldn't be surprised if, by the end of summer, James was into a whole new identification thing. Only this time it would be with a historically famous lady killer like—

"Don Juan?" James had suggested.

Max shook his head, grinning. "Sure," he said. "Sure enough. Don Juan it is. This will be the summer of the Don Juan Project."

Only it had turned out to be the summer of the New Moon Lake instead; and until Diane Jarrett had shown up there'd been no reason to think that any part of the Don Juan Project was transferrable to the high Sierras.

Inside the west gate a path led down through a grove of old trees and leveled out to merge with the jogging trail that bordered Anzio Avenue. After curving past two cabins, Anzio ran into Bunker Hill Road and directly down to the center of The Camp. On the jogging trail James shifted from the swift silent tread of the woodsman to a jog—when in Rome—and in a very few minutes was in sight of the complex of buildings grouped around a central quadrangle known as the "Parade Grounds."

There was no sign of Diane Jarrett in the Commissary, where James purchased bread, milk and half a dozen other items that Charlotte had added to the list at the last minute. There was no one of interest on the tennis courts either, or in the pavillion snack bar, or at the post office. In fact, at this hour of the day, nine thirty A.M., very few troopers of any description were in evidence anywhere. It would appear that in this particular military establishment reveille tended to be a bit late. But James persevered. Sometime earlier he had noticed a map on the post office wall—a map on which names had been inscribed at the location of each private cabin. Previously he'd had no particular interest in finding out who lived on which of T.J.'s favorite battlefields. But now, scanning the map eagerly, he located not one, but two cabins labeled with the surname, Jarrett. Above Cabin sixteen *The Duncan Jarrett Family* had been inked in, and on the neighboring premises, *Hank and Jill Jarrett and Family*. Both sixteen and seventeen were on Gettysburg Road, not far from the end of Anzio.

Considering the possibility of a different route home —one that included a tour of Gettsyburg—James was studying the map when the sound of running feet made him turn towards the window. A group of joggers was passing the post office; and judging by a split-second glimpse of a provocative profile, one of them might be the object of his quest. Collecting his sack of groceries, he shot out the door and into the Parade Grounds in time to see the joggers come to a stop at the sidewalk service window of the snack bar. Quite suddenly, it occurred to him that he was very thirsty.

There were four of them—four blond, sturdily trim and damply glistening joggers. Thick, snowy white socks hugged their ankles and terrycloth sweat bands in colors that matched their jogging suits encircled their wrists and brows. And one of them was, indeed, Diane Jarrett. One was a tall, thick-chested man, another was a sturdy-looking middle-aged woman, and the fourth was a young man who was probably in his late teens. While the older man ordered at the service window, the others walked in circles, panting and gasping; but when the drinks arrived, they all subsided around one of the sidewalk tables. To James, now crouching behind a Dr. Pepper at an indoor table, they seemed to be surrounded by a kind of aura.

Diane and the man and woman, probably her father and mother, were talking animatedly between diminishing attacks of panting and studying their wristwatches and the pedometers strapped to their ankles. The young man, however, only sat quietly, leaning back in his chair, his eyes staring blankly in the general direction of the lake. He was definitely, James decided, Diane's brother—or else gay. There couldn't be any other explanation of the fact that he was staring at the lake while sitting next to a glowing, panting Diane, whose chest, under her tight sweat shirt was still heaving in a really remarkable way.

Something suddenly interfered with James' line of vision, and he refocused to find himself eye to eye with

Fiona, the young Englishwoman who worked in the snack bar. Fiona, probably in her mid-twenties, was lean and bitter. She was bitter about England, America, the older generation, the younger generation, The Camp, T. J. Mitchell and the fact that her visa was going to expire at just about the time the weather got really bad in London. James found her even-handed disillusionment vaguely inspirational—an indication that prejudice was not inevitable, except perhaps against life itself. In the past he'd enjoyed chatting with Fiona, but at the moment she was refilling the sugar bowl on his table and in the process blocking his view of the outside world.

Leaning around her and pointing he asked, "Do you know who those people are?"

Fiona glanced wearily over her shoulder. "That lot at the table? Do I know that lot? Better than I'd like to, I can tell you."

"Why? What's the matter with them?"

"Oh well, it's not just the four of them out there, is it? It's the other one I could do without. The little one. Baby-sitting they call it. Well, let me tell you, there's not much sitting to be done. Dodging would be more like it."

Suddenly he knew what she was talking about. "Oh, you mean Jacky?" he asked.

"That's the one. Good name for him, too. Another Jack the Ripper, someday, I wouldn't be surprised." Fiona was wiping up spilled sugar so fiercely that the table jittered.

Deftly rescuing his Dr. Pepper, James asked, "You mean you baby-sit at the Jarrett's?"

She sighed. "Regularly," she said. "Every Saturday night."

"You'd think one of them could do it sometimes," James said sympathetically. "One of the other kids, I mean. They look old enough."

"You would think so, wouldn't you. But, oh no, not a bit of it. All four of them have to go out every Saturday night. The cook won't do it, either. Got it written right into her contract when she went to work for them, good job for her. No baby-sitting." Fiona was sounding bitterer by the moment.

"Well, why do you do it if you hate it so much?" James asked. "They couldn't make you do it."

She sighed. "It's the money," she said. "I'm helping my mum buy a new flat in Camden Town, and the Jarretts do pay bloody well, I'll say that for them." She glanced over her shoulder. "I make more money dodging Jacky for three hours than that old skinflint Mitchell pays me for a whole day." Still sighing, Fiona retired behind the counter.

When James noticed that the Jarretts were preparing to leave, he stood up abruptly, put his glasses in his pocket, reconsidered, sat down again and put his glasses back on in order to watch them jog away. When they were out of sight, he asked Fiona where they lived. "I know it's on Gettysburg," he said. "Is it number sixteen?"

"Sixteen? No, that's the other Jarretts. The Duncan Jarretts. The Dunkin' Jarretts, I call them. Always in the water. This lot's the hunting Jarretts."

"Hunting? What do they hunt for?"

"What don't they? You should see the poor things hanging around the walls in that cabin of theirs. Cabin!" She rolled her eyes upward. "More like a bloody castle. They have this room they call the trophy room that's bigger than most people's houses. That's where they keep most of the dead animals." Suddenly Fiona's eyes narrowed thoughtfully. "You have some particular interest in . . ." She paused, grinning. "Oh, so that's it, is it? Diane strikes your fancy?"

James started to say something about a casual meeting on the beach, but Fiona interrupted. "You'd better watch your step with that one, laddie. Wind up hanging over the mantle with the zebras, you will."

He left the snack bar soon afterward, discovered he'd left his groceries under the table, went back for them and left even more quickly with Fiona's bitter chuckle following him out the door. At the crossroads he bravely took Gettysburg Avenue, but although he walked very slowly past number seventeen, a palatial cabin completely surrounded by multilevel decks, no one was in sight. Defeated, at least temporarily, he took the footpath to Anzio and headed toward the west gate.

He was almost through the grove of old trees when he heard the sound of a high-pitched voice. He stopped and stood still, listening. The voice came again. "Grif. Griffin. Where are you?" A moment later a little girl, perhaps six or seven years old, bounded into view, saw James and stopped with a startled gasp.

She was small and dark, and her hair hung in jagged wisps around her narrow face. There was something about the aristocratic sweep of her long delicate nose that reminded James of a beautiful Afghan hound he had once been acquainted with. Like the Afghan, the little girl seemed to be suspicious of strangers. Backing away among the trees, she was staring at James with large, startled eyes.

"Hello," he said, smiling in what he hoped was a reassuring manner. "Did you lose—something?" "Grif" sounded like a pet, probably a dog.

Still backing, the girl continued to regard him warily. A moment more and she would probably have disappeared, but just at that moment the paper bag tore. A milk carton bounced off his foot, and as he grabbed for it, a loaf of bread shot out the top of the bag. While he was busy juggling groceries, he thought he heard a giggle, and when he was finished, with everything arranged more or less at random on the ground in front of him, except for one long strip of bag paper, which he still clutched in his left hand, he found that she had returned. Apparently the impromptu clown act had convinced her that he wasn't dangerous after all. Squatting in front of him, she gathered up fallen groceries and asked questions.

"Who are you? Do you live here, in The Camp? Have you seen a girl—a big girl in a shiny dress?"

James grinned. "My name is James. No, I don't live here, I just come here to shop at the Commissary. No, I haven't seen anyone around here. Except you, that is. What's your name?"

"Laurel. I'm Laurel Jarrett."

"Jarrett?" James' interest multipled geometrically. "Is the girl you're looking for Diane?"

In the midst of helping James stack his arms with loose groceries, Laurel Jarrett paused. Looking up she puckered her small mobile mouth as if she'd tasted something sour. "No. Not Diane. Diane is my cousin. Grif is —Griffin Donahue."

On the little girl's thin dark face vivid dramatic expressions came and went like colors in a kaleidoscope, and there was something about the way she said Griffin Donahue that was almost reverent. "Don't you know Griffin?"

"No, I'm afraid not."

"Shhh!" she said suddenly, her finger to her lips. For a few seconds she parodied listening and then disappointment. Concern, anxiety and deep, dark foreboding followed each other across her face in a way that would have done justice to a heroine in a silent movie. "I've got to find her," she said, making it sound as if it were at least a matter of life or death. "She said she'd be here."

Running on tiptoe she disappeared among the trees, and James, still clutching precariously stacked loaves and cartons, headed for home. A few seconds later he heard, faint but clear, a faraway echo. "Griffin! Griffin! Where are you?" There was something about it that was almost eerie.

CHAPTER 3

HE WAS hurrying, dodging around people on a crowded sidewalk. It was terribly important that he get there in time, and there wasn't a moment to lose. A large woman stepped in front of him, and he sidestepped, but not quickly enough to avoid brushing against her shoulder. Turning toward him, her face registered displeasure—and then shocked horror. He looked down at himself and saw with dismay that he was stark naked. You can't fool me, he told himself, this is just another one of those dreams. It was getting to be almost monotonous. But still, just to be on the safe side, he looked around for cover and shot into a handy doorway. He found himself in a large empty hall. Backing away from the glass doors of the entry, he bumped into a table and sat down on it. "May I help you?" a voice said, and he turned to find Diane Jarrett sitting behind the table. She was wearing the pink bikini. He'd been right about the dream. Here we go again, he thought.

As soon as he was fully awake, he got quickly out of bed. It was getting to be a bit embarrassing, even though Charlotte, who had always been very frank and matter-of-fact about such things, assured him it was a perfectly normal part of puberty. Which was all very well, except he still wondered if he wasn't overdoing normalcy a bit lately. It did seem that a person with universal goals ought to guard against getting into a rut. He grinned, thinking what Max would do with that one. Fielding, the natural-born straight man.

During breakfast that morning, he decided to take up tennis again. He'd attended a tennis class as a kid, at Charlotte's urging, and stuck with it for several years, progressing from terrible to mediocre. Though he hadn't played much recently, it suddenly occurred to him that this would be a good time to get back on the courts. It would, that is, if he could get permission from T.J. to play at The Camp. He didn't know why he hadn't thought of it before. Diane played tennis, for one thing, and for another he obviously needed the exercise. The question now was, had he remembered to bring his racket. He vaguely recalled packing it, but he hadn't seen it since they'd been in the cabin.

His mother and father had been engaged for some time in a very animated conversation regarding Disraeli and Queen Victoria, so he waited until there seemed to be a lull before he asked if anyone had seen his tennis racket. William stared at him blankly for a moment and then frowned. He'd lost track of the point he'd been about to make, he said, and was the whereabouts of a tennis racket a matter of such great urgency that it justified the interruption of a conversation?

James said he was sorry, but his father went on frowning. In the Fielding catechism, interruptions had always been one of the seven deadly sins. There wasn't any use trying to explain. Although it just might be argued that what could happen to him in the next day or two, if he could find his tennis racket, was somewhat more urgent than something that happened to Disraeli over a hundred years ago.

After his father remembered the point he'd been about to make, he made it at some length, and when he had finished Charlotte said she was glad that was settled, and if James would look on the top shelf of his closet it might settle another matter, too. A few minutes later he was on his way to The Camp completely equipped for a game of tennis.

When he entered T.J.'s outer office, Lieutenant Carnaby was feeding the fish in a whole row of small aquariums built into recesses all along one wall. She was in uniform, the belted khaki tunic over longish shorts that were regulation dress in T.J.'s army. It was probably supposed to look dashing and romantic—Her Majesty's officers on far-flung frontiers, or characters from a Hemingway novel—but the Lieutenant was short, frizzy-haired and shaped something like an old-fashioned milkbottle. The overall effect was pretty incongruous.

"Hello," she said, backing out of a tank recess and tugging at the skirt of her tunic. "Fielding, isn't it?"

"Yes, sss . . ." Uncertain about sir-ing a female officer, James let his salutation sizzle into silence.

"Did you want to see the major?"

"Not particularly. What I mean is, maybe you can tell me what I want to know. I just want to know if our Willowby pass gives us other privileges besides the use of the Commissary and the snack bar. Like the tennis courts, for instance? I mean, would it be all right if I came over now and then to play some tennis?"

The lieutenant frowned. "Well, I don't believe that situation has come up before, so I just don't know what the major would say. I think perhaps you'd better talk to him."

James had been afraid of that. The major, it seemed, was in. In a few minutes James was standing at attention in front of the major's enormous desk. He didn't want to, but he couldn't seem to help himself. In fact, everything in the room seemed to be standing at attention, including all the objects on the major's desk and the hair on his closely cropped head. His khakis were immaculately pressed and his lean, freshly shaved face had an almost metallic gleam. "Good morning, Fielding," he said. "What can I do for you?"

When James had explained what he wanted, the major got up and took some papers from an elaborate filing system and studied them carefully before he answered. "You realize, of course, Fielding, that in making a decision such as this, I must give first consideration to the needs of Camp residents." He paused and looked at James sternly. James nodded, wondering if that meant "Forget it."

"However," the major went on, "I see by our Facilities Use Records that the courts have not been fully utilized lately, so perhaps some of our tennis regulars would enjoy having a new adversary. Some fresh blood, as it were."

James considered saying he hoped it wouldn't come to that. Instead he diplomatically admired the view from the office window and an assortment of rifles in an enormous gun case behind the major's desk, while the files were being returned carefully to their proper place and a notation made on the back of James' pass, to the effect that it had been extended to cover use of athletic facilities. It was a very successful stratagem—the major handed back his pass with what came fairly close to being a smile, and then personally escorted James back out through the outer office, pointing out other items for him to admire. Carried away by the success of his diplomacy, James fervently admired a bright green plastic tree, an enormous photograph of The Camp's main entrance, and each one of the fish individually. They all looked pretty much the same. They were, the major said, belligerent little devils called Siamese fighting fish, which had to be kept in separate tanks to keep them from tearing each other into bloody scraps. By the time James left, he had been called upon to admire nearly everything in the office except Lieutenant Carnaby.

On his way to the tennis courts he stopped off at the snack shop to retrieve his racket and balls, which he had left with Fiona while he presented his case, not wanting to give the impression of overconfidence. He chatted for a while with Fiona, who was being bitter about the beautiful weather. It couldn't be like this on her day off, could it? Oh no. Let her take the day off and the thermometer automatically dropped twenty degrees. But just let her be stuck behind this counter and look at it. Paradise.

James sympathized and, rather guiltily, headed for the tennis courts, detouring once more at the pavillion's public restrooms; where it occurred to him to wonder if his use of the men's room would be officially entered in the major's Facilities Use Records.

On the courts, the only other person waiting for a partner was a ten-year-old boy, which wasn't too unfortunate, since James was so rusty. He even managed to win the second game. Then the little kid and a couple of other players went home to lunch. The one remaining player on the courts strolled towards James, bouncing a ball on his racket. He was tall, good-looking, blond and probably a year or two older than James—and suddenly James knew where he'd seen him before. He hadn't really observed him too carefully at the time—his mind, and eyes, having been on other things—but he was fairly sure that the guy was one of the jogging Jarretts. The one who was probably Diane's brother.

"Hi. Want to play a game?" The invitation was given in a tone of voice that indicated complete indifference, one way or the other.

"Sure," James said. "I'm pretty rusty though. You'll probably annihilate me."

The blond kid shrugged and headed for the far court. "My name is Mike," he said over his shoulder. "Mike Jarrett."

"I'm James Fielding."

Nothing more was said for some time except for game calls and a few four letter comments on faults and misses. Mike was, as James had expected, much the better player; but after the first few games James was able to give him enough competition to make things interesting. Like his sister, Mike had a sleekly sturdy build and moved with smooth control, but he played a lazy and not particularly aggressive game, as if he didn't really care about the outcome. Even when he faulted, you got the feeling that his muttered expletives were more for form's sake than for any real anger at himself for messing up. After the third set he said he'd better be getting home.

"Me too," James said, gathering up his equipment. As they left the court together and strolled across the bivouac area, he asked, "Do you spend much time here, at The Camp?"

"Yeah, quite a bit. Most of the summer and during vacations in the skiing season. And last year my dad took us out of school for a week during the hunting season, and we came up here."

"Does your dad commute to work or does he have the summer off?"

"Well, you might say he commutes. His offices are in Sacramento, and during the summer he's usually only here on weekends. He and my uncle have a plane and they fly up on Fridays and spend the weekend. Sometimes the rest of the family flies back with him, but usually we stay at The Camp during the summer. How about you? You visiting someone here? I mean, you're not a regular resident are you?"

James explained about the Willowby pass. Then he started describing his visit to T.J.'s office, being amusingly satirical about Lieutenant Carnaby's shorts and about how T.J. probably waited until no one was around and then put a couple of the fighting fish in together and thought brave macho thoughts about moments-of-truth and death-in-the-afternoon, while they chewed the fins off each other. Some of it Mike didn't seem to get, but he did grin a few times. When they got to the beginning of Gettysburg Road, James turned up it, too.

When Mike looked at him inquiringly, he explained about the footpath from the end of Gettysburg to Anzio, and how it was one of the routes he sometimes took on his way home. At the driveway to number seventeen, when Mike started saying good-by, James said, "Do you suppose I could get a glass of water? I'm dying of thirst."

"Sure," Mike said. "Come on up to the house." As they turned up the long drive, James felt his heart shift into high gear, which, of course, was not a good sign. It probably meant that his brain was, as usual, getting ready to go into atrophy. It was really discouraging, since he'd almost been able to convince himself that it wouldn't happen again. Not with Diane, anyway. Not after he'd already managed to hold a fairly normal conversation with her that day on the beach. But it had been Jacky who had made the difference then, by golf-balling him out of his usual self-conscious seizure and then by giving him something else to talk and think about—and he didn't suppose he could count on Jacky's clobbering him again today. For a moment he wished, or almost wished, himself out of the whole situation and on his way up Gettysburg Road toward the west gate and home.

In front of the Jarrett's so-called cabin, a wide flight of stairs with rustic log bannisters led up to the first level of decks, but Mike led the way around to the back. At the rear of the house they crossed a patio paved with redwood rounds and furnished with all kinds of fancy outdoor chairs and lounges. In the large kitchen, quarry tile floors and rough-hewn wooden cabinets attempted to preserve the myth of the simple life in the face of such contrary evidence as a built-in barbecue grill, a microwave oven, a trash compactor and a refrigerator that belched ice cubes through a hole in the door. By the time the ice avalanche was over, there wasn't much room in James' glass for water.

"Wow," he said to Mike. "Some kitchen."

Mike shrugged. "It's a kitchen," he said. "If you like kitchens. Would you like to see the rest of the place?"

James had heard about the trophy room from Fiona, but he hadn't really visualized it accurately. At least not in the proper scale. It was on the ground level, and it stretched from one end of the building to the other. Besides massive ceiling beams, an enormous fireplace, pool and Ping-Pong tables and a lot of leather furniture, it featured, just as Fiona had said, a huge assortment of dead animals. Parts of dead antelope, zebra, mountain goat, deer, moose, elk and buffalo hung from the walls, whole ducks and pheasants sat on shelves, an elephant's foot sat by the door holding umbrellas, a disembowled lion sprawled in front of the fireplace, and in the far corner, an entire polar bear crouched in perpetual rigor mortis. But deer seemed to be the Jarrett's popular victim. One whole wall was covered so densely with deer heads that it had the weird, almost surrealistic effect of dozens of pairs of sad dead eyes peering out of a wintry forest of antlers.

James was overwhelmed. He was even more overwhelmed a moment later when Diane emerged from the depths of one of the enormous couches. Kneeling on the seat of the couch, she leaned on the back and yawned lazily. "Hi," she said. "You woke me up."

"What are you doing down here?" Mike said. 'I

4 I

thought you went in to town with Mom."

"I decided against it. I came down here to read and went to sleep." Turning to James, she smiled breathtakingly. Pointing her gun finger, she said, "Ka-pow. Look who's here."

James and Mike rounded the end of the couches. Diane was wearing very short shorts and a tight brown tee shirt that said PLAIN BROWN WRAPPER across the front. There was a magazine on the couch beside her.

"Hi," James said, and then groping desperately for a conversational gambit, he picked up the magazine. "Is this what put you to sleep?" he asked.

The magazine was called *The Outdoor Man*, and the picture on its cover was of a man holding a rifle and wearing a day-glo orange vest and cap. He was smiling down at the body of a deer that lay at his feet.

Diane giggled. "Not really," she said. Taking the magazine out of James' hands, she pulled a copy of *Penthouse* out of the middle of it. "That's just camouflage, in case Dad comes in."

"Hey," Mike said grabbing the *Penthouse*. "Where did you find that?"

"In Dad's office. He thought he had them hid, but I found them."

"Hoo man!" Mike said. "Excuse me kids while I look at all the pretty pictures."

"Well, go away someplace. We don't want to be disturbed by all the heavy breathing."

Mike went off and flopped into a chair across the room.

"So how's your back?" Diane asked.

"My back?"

"Where Jacky nailed you."

"Oh that. It only hurts when I laugh." Hope sprouted. He'd said something. He'd even managed to be weakly funny.

She smiled encouragingly and hope burgeoned. "Speaking of Jacky," he asked, "is he around?"

"Why? Do you want to see him?"

"Well, not particularly. I just wondered if he was —within range."

"Relax. He went to town with my mom."

"Whew." Pantomiming relief, James sat down on the couch.

Diane's smile was welcoming—friendly—heart-splintering—mind-boggling. Giving a sudden little bounce of enthusiasm, she gestured around the room. "What do you think of our trophies?" she asked.

"Well," James said, "it's very impressive. I feel as if I ought to take off my hat. If I had one to take off."

"Well, don't take it off to me. I didn't kill many of them. Just a couple of lousy deer."

"Oh," James said. He decided against explaining that what he'd meant was more like—as in being in the presence of the dead.

"My dad wouldn't take me when he went to Africa. He said I was too young. He took Mike though, and he's just a year and a half older. But I've been going deer hunting since I was twelve years old. Come here, I'll show you." Getting off the couch, Diane led the way to the deer wall and pointed out two of the smaller heads. One had three points on each antler and the other had only two—probably a teen-ager as deer went —and they went fast, obviously, if they got within range of a Jarrett.

The tour continued with Diane telling James where each of the animals had been killed and by whom. Most of the killing had been done by her father.

"But my dad says I'm going to be a really great hunter someday," she said. "A lot better than Mike. Mike is still a little better shot than I am, but he just doesn't really care that much about it. Dad says he just doesn't have the desire."

"The desire?"

"Yes, that's what you have to have, to be a great hunter. My dad has it, and so do I. Mike just doesn't have it."

Glancing over at Mike, who was still avidly perusing *Penthouse*, it occurred to James that he seemed to have his fair share, at least in some areas.

"My dad says," Diane was going on, "that it's a shame they don't have an event for hunters in the Olympics. Don't you think they should?"

"Well, I guess I've never really thought about it," James admitted, picturing a football field full of milling deer and a bunch of hunters running around the track taking potshots at them. "They could have a deer shooting contest and a pig sticking and maybe even a rabbit thumping."

Diane looked at him coldly. "Okay, funny boy," she said. "I meant shooting at targets."

"Oh sure," James said. "I was just kidding."

She smiled angelically. "Ka-pow," she said, shooting James through the heart with a tan finger. "Don't try to kid me, sweetie. Hey! Do you like to play Ping-Pong?"

James was usually fairly good at Ping-Pong, but watching Diane jumping around at the other end of the table was hard on his powers of concentration. But he was having a wonderful time. He kept wishing that Max could see him now. Here he was playing Ping-Pong and kidding around with just about the sexiest girl he'd ever seen in his whole life. Max would be proud of him.

"Hey, Di," Mike called suddenly. "Was that a car?"

Diane ran to the window. "It's Mom," she said. "Mom's home."

Mike got up and put *Penthouse* under the cushion of his chair. A few minutes later the healthy-looking blonde woman came in. When Diane introduced James, Jill Jarrett was cool but friendly. She said that Di had to go down to the pool now for her diving lesson, but that she hoped James would come again. Diane walked out to the deck with him as he left. As he turned to go down the stairs, she made a little mouth at him like a kiss and he almost fell down the steps.

He was still walking on air as he went around the corner of the house and became aware of a rhythmical thudding noise. When he saw what was making it, he backed up and made a wide detour. It was Jacky. Dressed in pale blue overalls with bunnies on the front, he was busy squashing something with a toy shovel. He didn't notice James as he tiptoed past.

CHAPTER 4

HAVING discovered that diving lessons were on Fridays as well as Thursdays at three o'clock, James was at The Camp on Friday afternoon. At about three-thirty he wandered over to the swimming pool. He bought himself a Dr. Pepper from the vending machine and then ensconced himself in a plastic chair in the spectator's area. The only other spectators were two women who obviously were mothers of some of the kids in the class. They were watching the proceedings and drinking margueritas and discussing competitions and meets and the effectiveness of various coaches, and how their kids were absolutely determined to be Olympic competitors even though they'd never been pushed or coerced in any way.

There seemed to be only five kids in the class: Diane, a boy about fourteen years old and three girls who were quite a bit younger. The other kids were practicing on the low board, but Diane was diving from the high one. Although the coach, a very tan middle-aged man, yelled at her a lot, it seemed to James that she was very good at what she was doing. At least everything she did was very impressive to look at. However, Diane Jarrett in a bathing suit was very impressive to look at even when she wasn't doing anything. She was wearing a one-piece, light-weight tank suit of some clingy material, and while she climbed the ladder, poised at the top, jumped up and down and then fell in various graceful positions into the water, James had a perfect opportunity to make observations and check her off on Max's girl-rating scale. On Max's scale you rated various attributes on a scale of one to ten, and he was very particular. Not very many girls rated a ten on more than one or two points.

James grinned, thinking what Max could do with that one. Fielding the straight man. Max had said once that the reason he associated with James was because he was such a genius at setups. Of course, he'd been kidding at the time, but James had wondered if there wasn't some truth to that comment. James hadn't had a great many close friends in the past, and the ones he'd had had tended to be interesting and sharp, but on the whole a bit reserved and conservative. Not at all like Max. And from things Max had said, he'd gotten the impression that Max hadn't had many friends like James either. If James' contribution to Max's life was straight lines, Max's contribution to his was definitely excitement. On a scale of one to ten, Max rated at the top in making life exciting. And on Max's favorite scale, Diane Jarrett was obviously ten or close to it on everything from tits (super plus ten) to something Max called approachability. When her lesson was finished, Diane actually approached James.

She came out of the dressing room area and strolled

straight over to where he was sitting, swinging her beach bag and her hips. When she got there and pointed her finger, James actually chimed in on the, "Ka-pow." He was really making progress.

"You looking for somebody?" she asked in the special way she had that was sarcastic and seductive at the same time.

"Well, actually, I'm here on business." Better and better!

"On business?"

"Yeah. I'm on a stake-out." And then it happened —a line that even Max would have been proud of. "Actually, I'm from the FBI, and I'm keeping an eye on someone on the most wanted list." He even managed to raise an eyebrow when he said "most wanted."

Diane giggled, and a minute later she asked him to walk home with her.

While the line about the FBI was probably the highpoint, conversationwise, things continued to go well. When she asked him why he was taking off his glasses, he explained that he didn't wear them very often—only when there was something *really* worth watching—and she giggled again. Later he offered to carry her beach bag and she refused on women's lib grounds, and he insisted and tried to grab it, which led to some very exciting chasing and pushing and shoving. Eventually she put the bag behind her back so he had to put both arms around her to try to reach it, and at that point something more might have happened, except that they were in front of the Jarretts' cabin by then and all of a sudden a deep male voice called, "Diane." When James recovered from almost doing a back flip, he saw that the person who had yelled was a man who was sitting in a lounge chair on the bottom deck, smoking a pipe. Obviously it was Diane's father, and of course James had to go up and be introduced.

Actually, he wasn't too nervous about meeting Hank Jarrett, because all of his life he'd been good with adults. A lot better, in fact, than he sometimes was with people his own age—a situation which can result from growing up in a relatively adult environment. But Diane's father turned out to be a slightly different proposition. For one thing, Hank Jarrett talked mostly about three subjects, in none of which James had any particular expertise: building shopping centers, killing things and winning trophies. But there was more to it than that. The usual conversation gears just didn't seem to mesh. The whole process, question–answer, give–take, didn't seem to apply.

Right after Diane introduced James and said he'd walked up with her from diving class, her father said, "Diving class. What do you think of Fraser? Good coach, isn't he?"

"Fraser?" James had no idea who Fraser was.

"That Clifton woman," Jarrett went on without noticing James' confusion, "didn't know beans about coaching advanced divers. Can't think why Mitchell hired her. Okay as a swimming coach, I guess, for the kids just starting out, but out of the question for divers of Di's caliber. When I found out about her, I hit the ceiling. Got Mitchell to do something about the situation. Kids with an investment like our Di's," he put an arm across Diane's shoulders, "years of training and practice, can't be expected to go all summer without proper instruction."

Having deduced that Fraser was the diving coach, and still assuming that he was being conversed with, since Jarrett was continuing to look in his general direction, James felt called upon to respond. "I'm afraid I'm not much of an authority on—" he began before Jarrett interrupted.

"Don't need to be an authority as long as you give it all you've got. Get in there and give it all you've got. Right Di? That's what our Di does, and that's what counts. Isn't that right?" Hank Jarrett's lean, firm face was creased into a lean, firm smile. "You taking part in the Sacramento meet next week, Fielding?"

"No, I'm not—" James would have gone on to explain that he wasn't a swimmer and that he had only been a spectator and not a participant in Diane's class, but somehow before he'd managed to get the misconception cleared up, he was being taken in to see Diane's diving trophies and from there to look at trophies of other types, including all the animal parts that Diane had already introduced him to.

The next fifteen minutes or so of conversation consisted of a lot of unilateral comments on the joys of hunting in general, on specific thrills occasioned by the deaths of several of the room decorations and with the relative merits of various body parts as far as their record book standings were concerned. Meanwhile, Diane was tagging along, poking James now and then and making funny commiserating faces behind her father's back, which made it even harder for James to keep his mind on the information he was receiving. He learned with varying degrees of attentiveness that the polar bear didn't quite make the book, that the elk had been within a few points of establishing a record, and that five of the large assortment of deer had nearly made it, but not quite. The whole roomful, it seemed, had died in vain. It was a sobering thought.

"Diane got this beauty when she was only thirteen years old," Jarrett was going on. "Handled herself like a veteran. I started her out on a twenty-two when she wasn't much more than a baby, and she took to it like a duck to water. A real natural with firearms, this girl."

Diane pantomimed a two-fisted quick draw and ka-pow at her father's back, and James looked away quickly to keep from grinning.

Mr. Jarrett was pointing up at a head with exceptionally large antlers. "My own personal record is this old bruiser," he said. "Nailed him just a few miles from here five years ago. Just look at that spread. That's almost twenty-five inches. And eight points is very unusual in this day and age, let me tell you."

James counted the points. He was quite sure his stag had a lot more although he'd never actually counted them, not realizing the precise number was of any special significance. Right about then he was distracted by a particularly intimate poke from Diane, and while he was still trying to recover, the phone rang. Hank Jarrett excused himself and hurried upstairs.

Diane sat down on one of the leather couches, and James collapsed beside her. She was sitting with her feet tucked under her and her back held very straight, so that the print on the front of her tee shirt was very prominent—and only inches away from his shoulder. Today her shirt was blue with large black print that said, "Don't Touch Me."

"Let's see," she giggled. "Where were we when we were so rudely interrupted?"

"Well," James said, "you had your bag behind you, and I was trying to get it."

"Like this?" She put both hands behind her back, which further accentuated the topography under the printed message. James leaned toward her and put both hands around to where the bag had been, which of course resulted in pressing his own chest against the message and bringing his lips to within a couple of inches of hers. For the space of two or three very pronounced heartbeats, he waited to see if she was going to pull away, but she didn't, and a moment later he leaned a little more and their lips touched. Her lips were warm and soft and a little bit moist and they moved a little under his. It was very electrifying, and it would have been even more so if he hadn't been slightly distracted by wondering if he was doing it right and if she could tell that he hadn't done it very often.

After a few seconds she pulled away. But she didn't pull very far away, and unlike Heather Rubenstein, she didn't ask him why he had wanted to do that. Instead she only smiled at him in that half-teasing, half-inviting way, and he was just leaning forward again when he became aware of a very disturbing noise: *whirr-thud, whirr-thud, whirr-thud*. It sounded a lot like a golf ball rolling down stairs, and unfortunately that was exactly what it turned out to be. The ball reached the floor and rolled across the room into a corner, and a moment later

Jacky came into view at the turn of the stairs. James got up quickly and went to stand with his back to a wall. Diane stayed on the couch, but she turned so that she was able to keep her eyes on her brother, too. Jacky followed the ball into the corner, picked it up and came back across the room. He stared at James, and James stared back. The frown was familiar.

"You'd better come back over here," Diane said. "If he misses you there, he might hit the picture window."

"Don't worry," James said. "I doubt if he'll miss."

But Jacky seemed to be in a particularly benevolent mood. After glaring at James for several seconds, he toddled over and glared at Diane, all the time passing the golf ball back and forth between his fat little hands, but not making any attempt to throw it. He had turned around and was headed back toward the stairs when he suddenly detoured toward Diane's beach bag, snatched out her bathing suit and increased his pace to a trot. Diane leaped to her feet and over the back of the couch in one swift, sinuous movement, raced after Jacky and snatched the suit away. Even then, although Jacky cocked his arm at her, he didn't actually throw the ball. Instead he only stomped up the stairs, turning to glare down at them every few steps.

Diane put her suit back in the bag and put it on top of the wet bar. "Yesterday he flushed one of my suits down the toilet," she said. "The little creep."

"I hope it wasn't the pink one," James said. "I really like that one."

"Do you?" She made her eyes innocently round as if she couldn't imagine why anyone would notice her in a few old scraps of silky pink. "No. It wasn't that one." She sat back and patted the couch beside her. James was on his way toward her when the golf ball started down the stairs again. That was the way things went for the next half-hour. Just when things began to get interesting, the golf ball would start down the stairs, followed by Jacky. The mood was pretty much spoiled because, even though Diane seemed to be able to ignore Jacky's presence, at times James found that he couldn't. It was impossible to concentrate on what was in front of him—even when it was Diane—when the back of him was expecting to be golf-balled at any moment. At last Diane got up off the couch and said impatiently, "Look. I'm starving. Why don't we go upstairs and get something to eat."

But there were problems upstairs, too. In a little room just off the kitchen, which seemed to be a kind of office, Hank Jarrett was still on the phone and sounding disconcertingly threatening. All the time Diane was getting out various kinds of edibles, her father's voice was bouncing off the quarry tiles and double-glazed windows and echoing back from the interiors of the rustic cabinets. Under cover of the roar, Diane asked, "Want some chips?"

"Sure. Thanks." Charlotte, who had a thing about empty calories, wouldn't approve, but if they'd done Diane any physical damage, it surely wasn't evident.

"—and tell that fathead Meyer, I'm prepared to sue his ass off—" echoed around them as they nibbled on potato chips and stared into each other's eyes. "Cheese bits?" Diane whispered.

"Why not?" James whispered back.

"And Steve. You get that information to Dunc before you go home. You hear me. It has to be today. Keep calling the office, and try the club. Try the goddamn club every fifteen minutes."

"He's talking to his lawyer," Diane said. "He usually yells when he's talking to his lawyer."

It didn't seem to bother Diane at all, but James found the whole scene a little unnerving. When Hank Jarrett finally came out of his office, his expression seemed strangely familiar. James found himself checking for a golf ball. Of course, there wasn't any, but James decided not to risk outstaying his welcome, anyway. So he thanked Diane and Mr. Jarrett for their hospitality and headed for home.

Diane walked with him to the end of the drive. When they got to the road, she stopped and leaned back against a tree—on the side away from the house. That time the kiss lasted a long time.

On the way home James made two important decisions. The first one was that he was probably in love, and the second one was that he was going to stop telling Max about Diane. At least he was going to stop telling him everything. It had been all right to make humorous daily reports when the whole thing had been only a part of the Don Juan Project—but now that his relationship with Diane had turned into something much more significant, the reports would have to end.

Thinking back over the letter he'd written to Max after he first met Diane that day on the beach, and even the one he'd written only last night, he felt a little bit disloyal. The thing was he'd been a bit sarcastic about Diane's enthusiasm for guns and hunting. In fact, he'd actually gone so far as to make a crack about dangerous romances and how he was developing a fellow feeling for the males of certain other species, such as the black widow spider, doomed by their biological urges to lethal pursuits. He saw now that the crack had probably been very unfair. Of course, a fifteen-year-old girl would be enthusiastic about hunting if she'd been reared by a hunting family. She probably just hadn't gotten around to thinking the whole thing through for herself yet. He'd have to discuss it with her a bit more. Possibly point out some of the irrational ideas connected with it. And in the meantime he would simply write to Max and tell him that he didn't feel it was right to be humorous at the expense of a very significant long-term relationship.

The next afternoon, when he called Diane from the booth outside the snack bar, she said, "Oh, I don't think you'd better come up now. We're awfully busy getting ready to go to Sacramento. We're leaving tomorrow, you know."

"Tomorrow. For Sacramento," James said, aghast.

Diane giggled. "Don't take it so hard," she said. "It's only for a week. We were going to go in a couple of days anyway, because of the swimming meet, but now Dad says he has to be there sooner because of some trouble with a planning commission or something. But we'll be back next week. I'll see you then, okay."

"Do you have to go?" James asked.

"It's a very important meet. We're all going. Our whole family and my aunt. My Uncle Duncan is going to be one of the judges. He's already in Sacramento, and the rest of us are flying down tomorrow. See you next week. Okay?"

"Sure," James said. "See you next week." He hung up the phone and went into the snack bar to drown his troubles in a Dr Pepper.

CHAPTER 5

As HE approached the entrance to the hidden valley, he became aware of an anxious, almost guilty feeling. He had not been there for more than a week, had not in fact given the valley and its magnificent occupant more than a few minutes thought. But now, as he made his way down the steep incline into the canyon, he suddenly identified his vague discomfort as being related to guilt.

How could he have forgotten so quickly and completely the thrill he had felt when, after days of quiet observation, he had realized that the deer had been aware of and accepted his presence. And now, after his week-long desertion, would he still be tolerated? Or would the valley be deserted, the deer gone forever? Increasing his pace, he slipped and slid down the last stretch of loose shale to the valley floor.

There was no sign of the stag in the first small grove, nor in the clearing; but in the heavy stand of fir near the spring, James came suddenly upon him. Although he bounded to his feet at James' approach, he stood his ground, his head held high, his delicate black muzzle twitching as he tested the air. Closer now than ever before, James could clearly see the caplike patch on his forehead and how the massive antlers, which had seemed only dark and heavy from a distance, were actually covered with what looked like gray-brown suede. Sweeping up and out to almost twice the width of his body, the antlers branched and rebranched into six separate points on each side. Twelve prongs in all.

An unpleasant association twitched at the back of James' mind—a sea of sad dead eyes in a forest of antlers. Irrationally, the twinge of guilt returned, as if the lustrous living eyes of the stag could look into his mind and see it too: the long wall hung with the remains of so many of his kind. Like him and yet—not really like. With a thrill of some unnameable excitement, James realized that there was nothing on the wall in the Jarrett's trophy room—not even the head that Jarrett had presented as his own personal record—that came even close in size and symmetry. This stag was obviously one in a million. A wise and noble prince of the forest.

Digging into his pockets, James took out an apple and several slices of bread. He put them on the ground and backed away slowly and carefully, taking care not to make any sudden sound or movement. He hadn't gone far when the deer moved forward to accept his offering.

The apple went first and then the bread. The deer chewed calmly, his lower jaw working from side to side. Between bites he regarded James thoughtfully. He was still watchful, but obviously less wary and suspicious. When the last scrap was gone, he turned with calm dignity and retreated into the shadows of the grove.

James went back then to his favorite observation post on the flat-topped boulder. For almost an hour he sat quietly absorbing the ongoing dramas of the wilderness community, the teeming life of what might seem at first glance to be a deserted valley—the naively joyous energy of large families of birds, the timid bravado of chipmunk rivals and the constant half-seen, half-sensed, life and death scurry of the tiny, many-legged things beneath the grasses of the valley floor. He was lying on his stomach with his head hanging over the edge of the boulder watching a small army of ants attacking an enormous beetle when some mysterious sensing, not connected to ears or eyes, told him to raise his head.

The stag had returned. No more than fifty feet from the boulder he stopped, looked in James' direction and then, lowering his head began, calmly, to graze. Now and then he raised his head, looked again and went on grazing. It was almost like a conversation.

It was a very strange thing. Even more remarkable when you realized that a buck that had lived so long in an area overrun yearly by hunters must be not only cleverer but also more wary than others of his kind. Was he unafraid now because he somehow sensed that James meant him no harm? Or had he, perhaps, always lived safely in this almost inaccessible valley and never needed to learn fear in order to survive?

But, of course, the valley wasn't really inaccessible. The western end of the small box canyon seemed to have been blocked off, probably centuries before, by a tremendous landslide, so that the only entrance was by way of the cliff above Peter's Creek. But although the narrow path, high up on the cliff face, was dangerous, it was not impassable. Where James had come, others could come. And then, too, it seemed likely that the food supply in the small valley would be insufficient in the dead of winter. It seemed most probable that the deer came to the valley by way of the path at certain times, at the times perhaps when tourists and hunters invaded the mountains.

There was no way of knowing for sure. What did seem true, however, was that this deer, James' noble stag, was wiser and cleverer than others of his kind. Wise enough not only to have managed to stay alive for a long time, but also to know that James was a friend. The thought was suddenly and surprisingly eye-tingling and throat-tightening. James blinked, swallowed hard and said out loud, "You don't have to worry about me, old man. I won't betray you." A little later, when he got to his feet, the stag raised its majestic head and watched with calm curiosity as James saluted, bowed, slid down off the boulder and headed for home.

It was only ten or fifteen minutes later that James first saw Griffin Donahue. He had reached the highest point of the trail across the cliff face, a slightly wider spot where he usually stopped to catch his breath and enjoy the view, when he was suddenly aware of a strange sound. Looking down to the creek bed, he saw a mystifying sight. Someone was standing on a large rock at the edge of the water. He'd never before seen anyone on that stretch of the creek, a place where the water ran swiftly in a series of small waterfalls and then dropped in a long cascade to the lake below. At times the rushing water probably filled the entire gorge, but now, in the dry season, there was a narrow strip of boulder-strewn land on each side of the stream. It was a place where one might expect to see a determined fisherman or an adventurous hiker, but the person who stood on top of the large dome-shaped boulder obviously wasn't in either category.

Dressed in a long, close-fitting sheath that shimmered as if it were spun from silver thread, the person on the rock seemed strangely elongated, her body too narrow for its height. With her arms outspread, she was standing so perfectly still that for a moment James actually wondered if she were alive, or only some strange statue or mannequin. But then she moved, lifting her head and tilting it upward, so that her face was more clearly visible—eyes closed beneath dark, sharply defined brows, wide cheek bones and a full-lipped mouth. The mouth was closed and seemed to remain so, and yet the singing went on, a high, clear wailing chant. Frozen to the spot in amazement, James felt the hair on the back of his neck begin to prickle.

Then suddenly, two more figures appeared from behind the boulder, and it all became, if not clear, at least explainable. It was some kind of game. Because these other two were obviously little kids, probably less than ten years old. They were plainly pretending to be involved in a ritual or ceremony of some sort. The first one, who seemed to be a boy, had a beach towel robe over his shoulders and was holding a large basket in front of him. The other was a little girl. James leaned forward, pushing his glasses back in place and squinting. The same girl, in fact, he had met in the grove near the west gate. The one who had helped him pick up groceries and who had said that her name was Laurel Jarrett. But now she was wearing something draped over her head and was carrying what seemed to be a large blue vase. The two kids walked in a circle and then approached the rounded rock where the silver figure still stood motionless. The mystery of the high-pitched chant was now solved. The kids' mouths were opening and closing in time to the plaintive wail that had made the back of James' neck begin to crawl.

When they reached the rock, the silver woman knelt suddenly and took the basket from the boy. Then she rose and, reaching into the basket, seemed to be scattering something on the surface of the creek. She was singing now, too, her voice soaring over the children's, a high, clear, floating sound. Kneeling again, she returned the basket to the boy and, taking the vase from the girl, poured something into the foaming water below the boulder. A moment later she slid down off the rock, and the three of them moved slowly, in single-file, toward the cliff. It wasn't until then that James noticed the cavelike crevice in the cliff face. When they had disappeared into the crevice, he hurried on across the cliff and down the long incline to the Peter's Creek crossing.

He moved more quickly than usual, pushing himself until he crossed the stream, where he slowed to a thoughtful amble and then stopped altogether. Here at the crossing, the creek was wide and shallow, but he could see where, only a hundred yards downstream, the water was already beginning to foam and tumble. It would be a long steep climb down to the cave where the mysterious ceremony was taking place. He started down the bank, stopped and sat down on a rock to think. What, he asked himself, was he thinking of? Going out of his way to spy on some kind of silly game. It was late, and he ought to be getting home. The internal argument was still going on when he heard voices and looked up to see the game players themselves picking their way among the boulders a few yards downstream.

Watching them approach, James began to grin. He saw now that what he had taken to be a willowy woman —sylph, wood nymph, river goddess, or whatever—was nothing more than a half-grown kid. A girl at the age when some people shoot up a lot faster than they fill out —like James, himself, for instance. Except that this girl was obviously a lot younger than he—no more than twelve, perhaps, or possibly thirteen. Her odd, full-lipped, cat-shaped face had seemed quite mature from a distance, but from closer range it was clearly the face of a child. And the front of the slinky evening gown— no doubt borrowed from her mother—hung in two silver flaps over her very flat chest.

The three of them had been carefully watching their feet as they picked their way over the rough ter-rain, but at last the little boy looked up, saw James and let out a loud gasp. "Hey look!" he said. "Look Grif. Is that him?"

The girl in silver stopped, looked up, gazed at James intently for an embarrassingly long time and then nodded. Still nodding thoughtfully, she turned her back and, pulling the kids close to her, began to whisper. A long thick braid of dark blonde hair hung down the middle of her back, and below the hem of her dress, a draggle of frayed-out silver thread, her feet were bare. Both of the kids were looking excitedly from her to James and back again. When she came on toward him, the boy and girl were close behind, peeking around at him as if he were some kind of exotic beast. The girl in the silver dress scrambled over a last large boulder, a fairly graceful maneuver considering the tightness of her skirt, slid down directly in front of him and made a deep curtsey.

"Welcome," she said.

Surprised into vocal paralysis, he could only stare in amazement as the two kids slid down beside her and did more or less the same thing—the boy bending stiffly from the waist, and the little girl, it was Laurel all right, pinching the sides of her blue jeans and curtseying. As she curtsied, Laurel said something that sounded like, "Welcome, Prince Person."

"No," the boy whispered loudly, punching her in the shoulder. "Not Person. Pwah-son. Pwah!"

"Welcome. Prince Pwah-son," Laurel corrected herself.

Without taking her eyes off James' face, the girl in silver said, "Poisson."

"Fish?" James said increduously. It was the first word he'd managed to say.

Laurel made a gasping noise, and she and the boy stared at each other, as if the fact that James knew a little French was, somehow, terribly significant. They nodded at each other knowingly, and then looked back at James, still nodding. But then Laurel's mouth flew open, and she stared at James in broad screen consternation. "Wait a minute!" she said. "I've seen him before. Griffin! I saw him already. He can't be Prince Pwahson.

I saw him in the Nymph's Grove—with some groceries." She stepped closer, her face registering suspicion, but her skepticism was clearly directed at James, himself, and not at the girl in silver; as if she had caught James in some crass attempt at impersonation. "Didn't I," she demanded.

"I confess," he said. "We've met before. Your name is Laurel Jarrett. Right?"

"Griffin?" Laurel was clearly demanding an explanation.

"Of course," the girl in silver said. "Enchanted people get to return to their original form for short periods now and then. Like the prince in 'East of the Sun and West of the Moon.' Don't you remember?"

"Oh, yes!" Laurel was now doing *sudden enlightenment*—round-mouthed and -eyed. But then her face clouded again. "But he'd been shopping," she whispered. "Do enchanted people—"

"Look, Laurel," the little boy said. Except for bigger ears and more freckles, he looked something like the girl in silver, and right at the moment he was looking fiercely indignant. "If you'd been eating nothing but bugs and mosquitoes for a hundred years, I'll bet you'd go shopping too, if you got a chance."

The bigger girl put one arm around the little boy and gave him a hug. Smiling at him she said, "Shut up, Woody. You and Laurel go on and wait for me where the path goes into the trees. I have to talk to the prince alone for a minute. Okay?"

The little kids went off slowly with much stopping and looking back and whispering. When they were out of sight, the girl turned to James and examined his face.

It was the kind of long level look that ordinarily made him feel very uncomfortable, only this didn't. There was something about this girl's strange-looking face that made mutual staring almost acceptable—a kind of open, unprejudiced curiosity that somehow invited a similar response.

"Hello," she said after a while. "My name is Griffith Alexandra Donahue. But usually Griffin. What's yours?"

James grinned. "Prince Fish," he said.

She looked delighted. "It's like this," she said. "One hundred years ago an evil witch enchanted you and turned you into an enormous trout. And one day while Woody and Laurel and I were watching you swim around in a deep pool, way down there almost to the lake, you spoke to me and asked me to break the enchantment so that you could be a prince again. So today we did it. We had a spell-breaking ceremony, and just before you disappeared, you told me that the spell was broken but you couldn't appear to us as a prince immediately because the witch was watching, but that you would very soon."

"Wow!" James shook his head, grinning. Watching Griffin's steady slate blue eyes, exotically tilted and hypnotically intense, he was almost ready to believe the whole story. "Okay," he said. "Got it. I'm a big fish, otherwise known as Prince Poisson. But maybe you ought to know that I've been leading a double life—or would it be triple? Anyway, my other alias is James. James Fielding."

She shrugged. "That's all right. So do I."

"So do you, what?"

"Lead a lot of different lives. A lot more than

three." She sat down on a rock and tucked up her bare feet. The long braid hung over one shoulder and down into her lap. The silver dress clung close to her thin, limber body, making her look a bit like a fish herself, or perhaps like a rather undeveloped mermaid. She stared at James thoughtfully for a moment before she said, "You want to know something funny? I knew it. The minute I saw you, I knew."

"That I'd go along with the gag?" James said.

"No," she said indignantly, but then she smiled. "Well, maybe that too. But what I meant was that you probably really are one. Or at least you were one once. Otherwise you wouldn't have understood."

"I was *what* once?"

"Like in another reincarnation. You probably were a prince in another reincarnation."

"Why not?" James said. Maybe that explained the Julius Ceasar and Alexander the Great hang-ups. "How about you? Were you ever a princess?"

"Me?" she said. "No, I don't think so. I think I've usually been animals."

"Griffin!" The kids were calling from further up the canyon.

She sighed. "Little kids. Sometimes I get very tired of little kids."

"How old are they?"

"Well, Woody is seven. He's my brother. And Laurel is just a few months older."

"And how about you? How old are you?"

"In this reincarnation?"

"Well, yes," James said. "Let's start with this one, anyway."

"All right. In this reincarnation I'm thirteen. But I'm actually a very old soul."

"I wouldn't be at all surprised," James said.

"Grif! Come on. We're hungry." Woody and Laurel had come back around the curve of the canyon wall.

Griffin uncoiled herself and stood up. "I guess I'd better go." She started towards the little kids and then, turning back to James, she curtsied again. "Good-by," she said. "See you."

Further up the canyon Laurel and Woody bowed and curtsied and then jumped up and down waving and shouting, "Good-by, Prince. Good-by Prince."

James waved back. After they'd gone, he sat on the rock for quite a while, composing a letter to Max in his head. Max wasn't going to believe this one.

CHAPTER 6

THE WAD of paper arched neatly, bounced off the rim of the wastepaper basket and fell to the floor. It was very strange, since he'd been writing poetry all his life, that now when something really important had happened—the kind of thing that had inspired poets down through the ages—he suddenly seemed to have lost his touch. Of course, most of his poetry in the past had been humorous and satirical and in a style that wasn't particularly suitable for what he had in mind at the moment. The trouble seemed to be that while what he was trying to express was incredibly exciting and original and significant at what you might call the gut level, it kept coming out at the verbal level sounding surprisingly ordinary and trite. He'd tried sonnets, triolets, ballad form, blank verse and anapestic pentameter, all with about the same results—another opportunity to practice basket shooting.

He sighed, and pulling Jenkin's *A Man for All Ages* across the desk, he opened it to page thirty-two, which was as far as he had gotten in a whole month at

New Moon Lake. He might as well get some work done on the da Vinci thing. There probably wasn't any new way to say what he had in mind anyway. After all, where could you go after "How do I love thee" and "My luv is like a red, red rose"?

There was a knock, and Charlotte opened the door. When she saw James at his desk, she paused in the doorway. In the Fielding family one didn't interrupt intellectual exercise unless it was absolutely necessary. "I'm sorry," she said. "I don't want to interrupt your train of thought."

"Don't worry," James said. "It's already derailed."

Charlotte glanced at the wads of paper in and around the wastepaper basket. "Having trouble with Leonardo?" she asked.

"Well, not exactly."

"Well, what I came in to say is that we're thinking about driving in to New Moon. Would you like to come along?"

"No, I guess not, thanks. Now that I've finally gotten started on this thing, I guess I'd better keep at it awhile."

As Charlotte was leaving, James suddenly said, "Mom." Charlotte had always been easy to talk to on almost any subject. At least comparatively easy, judging by what he'd heard about other people's mothers. But when she stopped and came back, he changed his mind. There just didn't seem to be any way to put his feelings about Diane into words without somehow trivializing them. "Oh, never mind," he said. "We'll talk about it later."

"I'm in no particular hurry, if there's something

you'd like to talk about."

"No. It can wait. Right now I'd better stick with Leonardo."

He didn't, however, stick with Leonardo for very long. When he heard the Volvo's motor starting up, he went to the window. William was just getting into the passenger side of the front seat. Charlotte was driving as usual. It wasn't that William was a bad driver. It was just that on longer trips he tended to start concentrating on some important issue and forgot to notice such minor details as stop signs or oncoming traffic. So Charlotte encouraged William to concentrate on his important issues and let her handle unimportant routines, particularly the ones that were potentially lethal. As James watched from his window, she deftly backed and turned the old Volvo and set off briskly down the narrow dirt road.

James went back to his desk, poked at the da Vinci notes, wandered out the door and down the stairs. It wasn't until he was in the front yard that he realized where he was heading. The week that the Jarretts were to have been in Sacramento wasn't quite over yet, but it was possible that they might have decided to come back a little early. And even if they hadn't, a game of tennis might be just what he needed to work off some tension and restlessness. In fact, right at the moment, a game of tennis would probably help the da Vinci more than anything else he could do. Relax his nerves and do great things for his powers of concentration. Halfway down the drive he stopped suddenly and went back to the cabin for his tennis racket.

He'd played one set with a middle-aged lady and

was sitting on the sidelines waiting for another partner possibility to present itself when he heard the sound of running feet on the path outside the courts. He turned around in time to see Laurel Jarrett dash through the gate, skid to a stop and then stand still, staring delightedly in his direction. He smiled, and she started toward him, balancing on the tips of her toes. In Laurel's case, tiptoeing seemed to have more to do with the state of her emotions, than with any desire to move quietly. When she was directly in front of him, she came down off her toes and said, "Hi!" Then, glancing around and lowering her voice she said, "Prince Pwah-son."

"Hi, yourself," James said, and then with a sudden surge of excitement, "Hey, are you back from Sacramento already?"

"Oh, I didn't go."

"But your mother and father went, didn't they. Diane said your father was one of the judges."

She nodded. "They went. But they left me here with Susie. She's my baby-sitter. They never take me when they go to swimming things because I'm the only one in the family who sinks."

"You—sink?"

"Yes," she said tragically. "It's awful. I have the wrong kind of bones or something. Jacky doesn't even sink as fast as I do, and he's only two."

It was a real disappointment. For a moment he'd been sure that all the Jarretts must have returned. But Laurel was still standing in front of him doing her tragic heroine bit. "That's too bad," he said. "About the sinking." He moved over to make room on the bench, and she scooted herself up beside him. She was wearing denim slacks and a flowered blouse. Her feet, in very small blue sneakers, swung back and forth about six inches from the blacktop. It really was too bad that they all went off and left her just because she couldn't swim as well as the rest of them. She obviously felt very bad about it. "I'm sorry you didn't get to go," he said.

"Oh, that's all right. I didn't want to. Besides, Griffin says it's probably just an enchantment. The sinking. She says as soon as she figures out the right spells, she's going to disenchant me and then I'll probably be able to swim better than anybody."

"Oh, that's great. Where's Griffin today? I mean, how come you're not working on some enchantment or other this morning?"

Laurel sighed. Tragedy had returned. "She can't. Woody has tonsilitis, and she has to take care of him."

"Where are their parents? Did they go to the swimming meet, too?"

"No. I think they just went to a party. They usually go to parties. Is it nice not being a fish anymore? Or do you miss it sometimes? The secret pool and everything. Griffin says it's not so bad being a fish as long as you're smart enough not to get hooked. Griffin says she was a fish once, and it wasn't too bad."

"Oh, well yes. I guess I'd say that Griffin was right. It wasn't too bad, most of the time." He grinned. "I did get tired of those mosquitoes though."

Laurel grinned back, her excited, lopsided smile. Slipping down off the bench, she picked up James' tennis ball and ran in a circle bouncing it. James went back to watching the other tennis players and wondering if anyone else was going to need a partner any time soon. It didn't look as if anyone was. When Laurel came back and scooted back up on to the bench, he said, "I guess I'm going to be leaving now. Say hello to Griffin and Woody for me when you see them."

"Okay." Laurel jumped down, and when James started off she ran along behind him, skipping and jumping and making a funny singsong noise. It was actually a little bit embarrassing, but every time he stopped and looked back at her she smiled at him lopsidedly, wrinkling her long, delicate nose and looking so pleased with herself that he couldn't bring himself to chase her away. But when he came to the beginning of Anzio, he said, "I'm going up Anzio now to the west gate. Where are you going?"

"I am, too. I'm going to Griffin's house. Griffin's house is number nineteen."

James remembered number nineteen. It was on the west side of Anzio, not far from where the trail began that led through the grove of pines to the west gate. So they went on together until they came to the driveway. The house, an immense A-frame set on a massive stone foundation, loomed over them at the end of a short, steep drive.

"Come on up and see Griffin," Laurel said, tugging at his hand. "Griffin hasn't seen anybody but Woody and me for two whole days." The tugging, along with a certain amount of curiosity, won. James allowed himself to be led up the drive and a flight of stone steps. Pushing open a sliding door, Laurel went in without knocking, and James followed. The living room towered, an enormous triangle of glass on one end, a stone fireplace wall on the other, and on each side huge sloping surfaces of rough-hewn wood. There was nothing in the room that actually looked like a piece of furniture. Vases and ash trays sat on white plastic mushrooms or clear glass cubes, books lined up along racks of chrome and glass, and in front of the fireplace was an enormous conversation pit, terraced in squashy velvet. On the walls and dangling overhead were several works of art that looked as if they'd been stolen from the opening sequences of *Monty Python's Flying Circus*. At the moment the room also was decorated with an assortment of toys, newspapers, articles of clothing and dirty dishes. Griffin, dressed in a Mexican-looking smock with faded embroidery around the top, was lying on her stomach on the lower level of the conversation pit. She was reading a book, and all around her were dozens of other books. When Laurel said, "Hi, Griffin, look who I brought to see you," she sat up quickly, looking startled.

"Hi," James said, "Laurel insisted that I come in. Hope it's okay."

A wide smile replaced the startled expression. "Of course, it's okay. Enter Prince Poisson and welcome. You honor our humble castle with your royal presence. You'll have to excuse the mess, though. My folks are away and our live-in left, and I'm a lousy housekeeper."

"Where's Woody?" Laurel asked.

"He's in his room. He still has a fever." Then, as Laurel started to run on tiptoe toward a doorway, she added, "Don't get too close to him. He might be catching."

James made his way down to the lowest level of the conversation pit, which was completely awash with what seemed to be very old books. Books were everywhere—stacked, tumbled, piled and scattered.

"What's been going on here?" he asked. "You been hijacking bookmobiles?"

"No. They're mine. I bought them. Aren't they great?" She slid down among the books and started gathering them into stacks, handling them as carefully as if they were valuable heirlooms. "They had a sale at the library in New Moon. Books people donated and all the old ones they didn't want any more. I bought them all. There were too many for me to carry, so yesterday Mr. Grant, he's the librarian's husband, delivered them for me. I'm going to read them all."

James picked up a couple that were lying near his feet. *Kiss Me Deadly* by Mickey Spillane looked as if it had been left out in the rain and Jane Austen's *Emma* had obviously been attacked by a dog. "Well, it looks like an interesting assortment," he said.

"Yes, I know. I just finished that one." She was pointing at *Emma*.

"Did you like it?" Charlotte had all of Jane Austen's books, and James had read a couple with rather mild interest.

"I loved it. I love all her stories."

"Oh. What do you like about them?"

"Oh, I don't know. They're just so perfect—and small."

"Small?" He examined the width of the book.

"I don't mean short. I mean small things happen. But it makes you understand how they didn't seem small to the people in the story."

Charlotte had said something not too different

when they'd argued about Austen. He was trying to remember just what it was, when something ran up his right leg. For an awful moment he thought it was a rat, a book carton stowaway from someone's attic. But it turned out to be a chipmunk. When it got to his lap, it grabbed the top of a pocket and tugged with tiny long-fingered paws.

"His name is Tad," Griffin said. "He just wants to see if you brought him anything. I usually keep sunflower seeds in my pockets."

The chipmunk sniffed in James' pocket, made a scolding noise and skittered across books to run up Griffin's braid as if it were a rope ladder. Perched on her shoulder, chattering impudently, flicking his striped tail, he seemed to be running on sixteen cylinders—bursting with too much life and energy for such a small chassis.

He's incredible," James said. "How did you get him to be so tame. I've tried to tame chipmunks and I've gotten a couple of them to come to within a few feet of me, but that's as far as it goes."

"I got him when he was just a tiny baby," Griffin said. "I'd been watching his mother, and I was pretty sure she had babies in a hole in a log. And then one day, right while I was watching, a hawk got her. It was terrible. There wasn't anything I could do except to get the babies out and see if I could help them, but they were pretty young, and two of them died. Tad was the only one that made it. He thinks I'm his mother." She reached into the pocket of her smock, took out some sunflower seeds and held her arm straight out in front of her. The chipmunk ran around the back of her neck to her other shoulder and then out her arm. When he got to her hand, he began stuffing seeds into his cheeks with both hands. With his cheeks bulging like a bad case of mumps, he ran back to her shoulder, down her braid and away across the room. "He's probably headed for my closet," Griffin said. "He's been storing up for winter in the toe of one of my shoes."

"Griffin. Can I get up now? I'm feeling a lot better." Woody came into the room followed by Laurel. He was wearing striped pajamas and his touseled hair had that faintly green tone that blond hair gets when it needs to be shampooed. "I want to talk to the prince, too."

"Woodrow Everett Westmoreland. You go right back to bed. You still have a fever." Griffin got up quickly, put her hand on Woody's forehead and then started leading him back down the hall. "Come on," she said. "Laurel can stay in your room and talk to you for a while if she doesn't get too close."

"Can the prince come talk to me, too? I want the prince to come talk to me." Twisting around so that he was walking backwards as Griffin tugged him along, Woody stared at James, his slate-blue eyes glittering with fever and self-pity. "I've been sick, Prince," he said. "And I'm awful bored. Being sick is awful boring."

So they all wound up sitting around in beanbag chairs and on a canopied wicker couch that hung from the ceiling in Woody's bedroom. The room, like the rest of the house, was fantastic. The bed hung from the ceiling, too, and it could be raised up during the day to make more play space. One set of controls was in the head of the bed so you could even make it go up and down while you were lying in it. Around the walls were built-in desks, bookcases, toy shelves and an enormous model train table. Very expensive looking toys were scattered everywhere. At first glance, you might wonder how a kid could be bored in a place like that, but after a while you began to understand. The place was boring. There was something deadening about all that slick, shiny, automated junk, most of which did all kinds of complicated things if you pushed a button or pulled a switch. The toys did it all. They rolled, walked, crashed, fought, beeped and talked. There was nothing left for a kid to do but lie there and watch. No wonder Woody was anxious to talk to somebody.

At first they talked about something that had been going on just before Woody got sick, something Woody called "helping the warfs." Sitting in the center of his touseled bed with his hair standing on end and his cheeks glowing feverishly, Woody went on at great length about some poor losers, mysteriously known as warfs. The warfs, it seemed, lived in some caves along the river bank and they'd been having a lot of trouble with a gang of goblins. The goblins had stolen the warfs' food supplies, and the warfs were about to starve when Grif found out about it. So she and Woody and Laurel had started helping by providing the warfs with food and anti-goblin magic and other necessities.

James caught Griffin's eye and grinned, but her answering smile was wide-eyed and earnest, without the slightest admission that she'd been putting anything over on the kids, and without any indication that she was asking him to back up her story. But he decided to, anyway.

"That's the way it goes everytime—with warfs and

goblins," he told Woody. "I've never known it to fail. You know—goblins ninety-nine, warfs zero."

"Not warfs," Laurel said. "Dwarfs. Woody just calls them warfs since his top teeth came out. But what they are are *dwarfs* like in Snow White." Laurel said *dwarfs* very distinctly, by pushing out her lower lip and curling the upper one up on one side.

"Sure," James said. "That's what I said—dwarfs. I never met a bunch of dwarfs yet who knew how to get the best of goblins. The thing with dwarfs is, they just aren't organized. What you ought to do is start a dwarfs' union. Start an organized protest. Picket lines, sit-down strikes, that sort of thing. That would take care of those goblins. I mean, what are they going to do when the goblin parking lot is full of limp dwarfs."

Griffin didn't smile, at least not with her mouth. Laurel and Woody gazed at James with undisguised admiration. When they looked at Griffin, she nodded solemnly. "I'll tell them," she said. "I'll tell the dwarfs what the prince said. It might help."

After that the conversation got really far out, all about enchantments and curses and talking animals and haunted forests. It wasn't too long before Woody began to run down. His eyes drooped, and he seemed about to keel over. When Griffin suggested he lie down and rest, he didn't argue. On their way back to the living room James asked, "How come he's Woody Westmoreland? Isn't he your brother?"

There was a difference in the tone of Griffin's voice as she answered. "He's my half-brother. We had different fathers. Our mother is Alexandra Griffith. That is, she was until she married my father." They'd reached the living room, and Griffin stopped to pick up a pair of blue jeans. She wadded them into a ball, clutched them against her chest and looked down at them instead of at James as she asked, "Have you heard of Alexandra Griffith?"

The definite difference in her face aroused his curiosity. "No," he said, watching her closely. "I don't think so. Why? Should I have?"

She shrugged. "I just thought you might."

Still wondering about the tight look around her eyes and mouth, he probed further. "But your name is Donahue?"

"Yes. My father was Kevin Donahue. He got killed in an accident, and after that my mother married Woodrow Everett Westmoreland the Second. Woody is the third."

"I'm sorry. About your father."

She shrugged again. "It was a long time ago. I can barely remember him. She was still looking down; and without being able to see her eyes, it was impossible to tell whether the tension in her face and voice was sorrow or anger or something else.

"Where are your parents now?" he asked, hoping to make her look up.

"In Reno. They go to Reno a lot when we're staying at The Camp. They have some friends there, and Wes, that's my stepfather, likes to gamble."

"Does he work there? In Reno?"

"No. He doesn't work anywhere, really. At least not very much. He has to go to San Francisco sometimes to see about money. His lawyer and stockbroker and people like that. But he doesn't really work."

"Do they know about Woody?"

At last she looked up. "What about Woody?" she said sharply.

"Do they know he's sick? It seems to me they'd like to be here until he gets to feeling better."

She turned away. "Oh that. That's all right. They knew he was sick. He gets tonsillitis all the time, and he always gets better after a few days. Usually we have a live-in who takes care of us when they go away, but the last one left and they couldn't get anyone new in time. But it's all right. Woody hates most of them. He'd rather just have me take care of him."

She walked to the glass wall and stood staring out, still clutching the wadded-up blue jeans, like a kid with a security blanket. James followed her, still trying to think of something to say that might change her mood. But the difference was still there, and it felt defensive now, suspicious, as if she were holding back, shutting him out as a person not to be trusted. Her surprisingly immediate acceptance of him as friend and fellow pipe dreamer was just as suddenly gone, and the more he tried to get it back by showing that he was interested and sympathetic, the more distant she seemed to become.

Suddenly, without more than a moment's consideration of the consequences, he found himself saying, "Hey. Would you like to see something really amazing? I found this secret valley . . ." He'd barely gotten started when he was sorry, when he knew it might be an awful mistake; but by then it was too late to stop. She was looking at him again, and her odd, oblong eyes were back to their normal high voltage.

"There's a deer," he said. "Not an ordinary deer—"

But just then Laurel came running down the hall. James shook his head. "Later," he said, but the die was cast, and before he left he'd told her all about the deer and promised to take her to see him.

That night, while he was helping Charlotte clean up the kitchen, he was thinking about it, about what he had done and about Griffin, herself—and the strange way she reacted to any mention of her parents.

"Have you ever heard of anybody named Alexandra Griffith?" he asked.

"Griffith?" Charlotte said. "Alexandra? Oh yes, of course. The Griffith heiress. I haven't heard much about her lately but back ten or fifteen years ago she was constantly in the public eye—newspapers, magazines, television."

"Why? What did she do?"

Charlotte, who could be very critical of people whose foibles she didn't approve of, curled her lip. "Nothing," she said. "As far as I can remember, not a damn thing. Except to have been born rich and beautiful, and extraordinarily uninhibited. She was just a debutante who went around doing shocking things and making scandalous statements to the press—mostly to get attention, no doubt. Then she got married. Ran off and married some playboy daredevil—raced cars and airplanes —something like that. For a while after that they were both in the news, but then there was an accident. If I remember correctly, the husband was killed and she just barely lived through it."

"Was his name Donahue?"

"I think it was, now that you mention it. How did

you happen to hear about them? It all happened years ago."

"Well, Alexandra Griffith lives at The Camp. Only she's married to someone else. Her name is Westmoreland now."

"Really?" Charlotte seemed to be quite impressed. "Did you hear that, William? That Griffith girl, well, woman now, is living—"

William, who was reading a book at the kitchen table, put a finger on his place and looked up, but you could tell by his unfocused eyes that he wasn't really hearing. "Never mind, darling," Charlotte said, "I'll tell you later."

She went back to the dishpan then, and James finished drying the pots and pans. But later, when he was on his way to his room, he made a sudden detour into the sunporch that William was using for a study and flipped open the dogeared *Webster's Unabridged*. Back in his own room he made a notation on a three-by-five card from his da Vinci file. "Griffin," he wrote, "also Griffon or Gryphon. A fabulous creature half-lion and half-eagle." After a moment he added, "Half daring debutante and half dead daredevil. Given to telling fantastic lies with great sincerity and the truth as if it were a dangerous secret." Then he filed the card under G.

CHAPTER 7

ACCORDING to Fiona, the Jarretts had returned. "That's right," Fiona said. "They're back all right. They all popped in here just at closing time last night. Ethel, that's their cook, wasn't due back from Reno until this morning, and poor Mrs. Jarrett was just too exhausted to make dinner." Fiona sighed and rolled her eyes in not too convincing sympathy. "Jogs for two hours without turning a hair, she does, but just let her catch a glimpse of a frying pan and she's as weak as a cat. So here they came just as I was trying to clean up and get home—all five of them. Jacky was in top form. Spilled his milk and had a go at the front window with his golf ball."

"Don't tell me he missed," James said.

"Not really. His mum grabbed his arm just in time."

"And what happened then? Didn't she take it away from him?"

"Take it away? Not likely. All she did was buy him two ice cream cones—one for each hand." Fiona shook her head grimly, but then suddenly she almost grinned. "Wish he had broken it. I wouldn't half-mind seeing the major and that Hank Jarrett having a real row."

James laughed. "Boggles the mind," he said. "I can see it all now. A kind of Snack Bar Armageddon."

Fiona actually chuckled. While she was still chuckling, James was out the door and poised in front of the phone booth. He squared his shoulders, breathed deeply several times and dialed Jarrett's number. Jill Jarrett answered the phone.

"Oh yes, James. Yes, of course, I remember you. The tall boy—brown hair."

"That's right. Mrs. Jarrett, I was wondering if . . . do you suppose I could speak to Diane?"

There was a slight pause. "Why yes, James. I should think so. Let me see if Di is available at the moment."

Then Diane's voice: high-pitched—very female—exciting. "Jamesy. We're back. Did you miss me?"

"All the time," James said, trying to keep his voice light and teasing the way she always did—so that you never knew if she meant it or not. "I've been pining away. Down to a shadow of my former robust one hundred and forty pounds."

She giggled. "Hey," she said. "Want to play some tennis?"

James would. A few minutes later he was at the court. It was another beautiful day, cool and sunny, and several people were there ahead of him. James sat down on the sidelines to wait. His favorite ten-year-old opponent came over and asked for a game, but James told him he was expecting someone else at any moment. About a half an hour later Mike Jarrett came in with another kid about his age, and when he saw James, he waved his racket. He and his friend took over the far court. It was at least another half hour before Diane showed up.

He saw her first when she was still halfway across the bivouac area, and not wanting to appear too eager, he sat down and looked the other way. He didn't turn around until he heard the squeak of the hinges on the court gate. He got up then and started toward her—and stopped in mid-stride. Slamming the gate behind her, she came striding toward him, sleek and tan and sexy—wearing a very short white dress and a flat-eyed, clenched-jawed frown. As she marched toward him, he felt himself tensing as if for a blow, but with a brief nod she swerved around him and went on down the court to where her brother was in the midst of a rally.

"Mike," she said. Mike missed the ball and everyone in the vicinity turned and stared. Mike went to meet her, and for the next several minutes the two of them engaged in a hunched-shouldered, clenched-fisted, squinty-eyed conversation. Mike's partner watched curiously from the center of the court, while James fretted, wondering if he should sit down and wait or go over and see if he could do anything. At last, he decided on the latter.

As he approached, Diane broke off the conversation and started toward him, and then whirled back suddenly towards Mike. Walking backwards she said, "Okay, just remember, Mikey. Next time . . ." Flipping her racket around she pointed the handle at her brother and made a machine gun noise. "Ack-ack-ack!" Twisting, she raked the muzzle of her racket-gun from side to side, flaring her short skirt over tight white shorts, and then turned and skipped up to James. "Brothers! she said, smiling dazzlingly. "Ugh!" and then, "Hi, sweetie. Want to play with me?"

"Sure," James said. "Any time. Any game."

She giggled and skipped over to the far court. They played for about an hour and then walked up to the Jarretts' cabin together. On the way she told him about what had been going on between her and Mike.

"He's a dirty traitor," she said. "Dad's been teaching us how to drive his new land-cruiser. It's really neat. Four-wheel drive and wide-track tires. It'll go almost anywhere. He bought it for hunting trips, and he's going to let Mike and me take turns driving it this season when we're out in the woods away from traffic. Only he won't let us drive it except when he's with us, which is really a dumb rule because I'm already very good at driving it. So anyway, last week when Dad was in Sac and Mom was down at the lake I took it for a little spin, and when I was turning around up at the end of Anzio I kind of backed into a tree. It wasn't my fault. The stupid contractor just didn't leave enough room up there for even a VW to turn around in. It wasn't much of a dent, but my dad never misses anything. So when he came storming into the house, Mike squealed on me. Just like that. So now I don't get to drive the cruiser for a whole month. Isn't that disgusting?"

"Why did he do it? I mean, why did Mike rat on you?"

"So he could learn to drive the cruiser better than I do. He said it was because Dad was blaming him, but the real reason is that he's always very jealous of everything I do. He's always been that way. He's just a very jealous person. Can you imagine anyone doing anything so cruddy? I mean, can you really?"

"Yes," James said, "I mean, no." The truth was, he'd gotten so engrossed in watching—in watching the curl of perfect lips over perfect teeth, the angry heaving of a perfect chest, the flashing gold-brown eyes—that he'd almost forgotten to listen to what she was saying. But now, getting the gist of the conversation, he hastily agreed that he couldn't and was rewarded by a quick kiss that turned into a longer kiss, and then a quick detour off Gettysburg and in among the trees, where there were several more kisses. By the time Diane twisted away from him and skipped back to the road, his chest was heaving as much as Diane's had been, but not with anger, and other parts of his anatomy were pretty much out of control, too. Fortunately when they reached the Jarretts' cabin things were just about back to normal, because Mrs. Jarrett and Jacky were in the trophy room when they walked in.

Jill Jarrett was in a friendly, or at least talkative, mood. "Well, hello, James," she said. "It is James, isn't it? Yes, I thought it was." Her intensely benevolent smile somehow made him feel as if he ought to be overwhelmed with gratitude at being remembered.

"Yes," he said with what he hoped was the proper amount of enthusiasm.

"Di," she said, "Barbie called a few minutes ago. I told her I'd have you call back as soon as you came in."

"Ooh, Barbie," Diane said. "I have to talk to her right away. It's very important. Excuse me just a moment, will you James?"

Diane ran up the stairs and James went on standing in the middle of the room. Mrs. Jarrett was sitting on one of the leather couches, and Jacky was doing something on the hearth in front of the huge fireplace. James couldn't make out exactly what, because his glasses were still in his pocket, where he had put them while he and Diane were in the grove. Feeling that nearsightedness was a handicap he couldn't afford in the present company, he got them out and put them on. Then he stood around trying to convince himself that he was relaxed and self-confident. He put his hands in his pockets, pulled them out, flicked a speck of dust off his shirt and glanced casually around the room—which made him feel more uncomfortable than ever. It was irrational, of course, but if you're feeling self-conscious, it doesn't help to be surrounded by dozens of pairs of staring eyes—even if the starers are only animals and dead at that.

James focused his attention on Jacky. Jacky was playing with two toy cars. One was a very large dump truck and the other was a tiny red sedan. Jacky was making the dump truck run back and forth over the sedan. He had hold of the dump truck with both hands, but there was a golf-ball-shaped bulge in the pocket of his coveralls.

"James," Jill Jarrett said, "do sit down. Di's apt to be on the phone for some time. Barbie's an old friend and a dedicated gossip. We're neighbors in Sacramento, but during the summer the girls keep in touch by phone." She smiled indulgently. "Our phone bills are disgraceful I'm afraid. My husband tears his hair, but what can you do with fifteen-year-olds?" Jill Jarrett's smile was sometimes very much like Diane's.

"Not much, I guess," James said, sitting down across the enormous free-form redwood-burl coffee table from Mrs. Jarrett and Jacky. There was no point in mentioning what Charlotte had done in a similar circumstance —after James' first long distance call to Max. What Charlotte had done was to suggest rather forcibly that from then on James and Max should carry on their summer dialogue by means of the United States Mail. Unless, of course, James wanted to use his own money. James didn't, since about two more calls would have used up his entire life savings.

James asked then about Mr. Jarrett—if he had had to go back to Sacramento already—and from there the conversation went to how hard Mrs. Jarrett's poor husband had to work and what a shame it was that he couldn't spend more time at The Camp since he really loved it, more perhaps than any of the rest of the family.

"He planned the whole house himself, you know," she said. "He worked with the architect from the very first sketches. This room was entirely his idea. Until the cabin was built, Hank never had a place to display all his beautiful trophies. At least not the kind of place they deserve."

Looking up at the head of an impala, James wondered briefly what it could have done to deserve Hank Jarrett's trophy room. It was an interesting thought, but he decided against sharing it with Mrs. Jarrett. She was still going on about hunting and how much it meant to her husband. "Are you interested in hunting," she asked James.

"Well, not really," James said. "I guess what it is,

is that I just don't really understand the—attraction, I guess you'd call it. I mean, I know that a lot of people really find it an exciting thing to do, but—well, I guess I don't really see what they get out of it."

Mrs. Jarrett smiled graciously. "Actually, I'm not much of a hunter myself, so I don't suppose I understand entirely, either. But you should hear Hank on the subject. On most topics he tends to be, well, rather plain spoken; but when it comes to the joys of hunting, he can be positively eloquent."

"The *joys* of hunting?" James asked in a very sincere, straightforward manner. It wasn't just that Jill Jarrett was Diane's mother either, and therefore a good person to be on the best possible terms with. He really was curious to know.

"Well. A lot of it has to do with being in the great out-of-doors. Exploring virgin country, sleeping under the stars, waking up to the smell of coffee and bacon over a campfire, and of course the special kind of close friendships that develop among a group of hunters out in the wilderness."

James nodded. "Okay. All that I understand. But why not just go backpacking, or if you want to hunt animals, why not with a camera?"

The explanation got rather complicated and confusing after that. It seemed that Hank didn't think much of camera safaris, but the exact reason never became clear. Basically, what it seemed to be was that you tended to meet a better class of people on an actual hunting safari; and although exactly what "better" meant was even less clear, what it boiled down to was—people with more money. James played it very straight and didn't make any of the humorous comments that occurred to him; but either Mrs. Jarrett sensed what he was thinking, or else that there were a few holes in her logic, because she began to sound a little bit irritated.

At last she got to the point where it came out that killing something was a very important part of the attraction. James said, "Well, maybe the problem is that I asked the wrong question in the first place. Maybe what I need to have explained is the joys of killing." At that she looked at him rather sharply.

Just about then Jacky began to pound on the red sedan with the poker, and Mrs. Jarrett had to get up and take it away from him. After she'd ordered him to leave the poker alone several times, she got up again and put it on top of the mantel. Then she lit a cigarette and started asking James questions about his family and the Willowby cabin.

"Well, wasn't it nice of the major to allow you to use The Camp facilities," she said. "Especially nice for Mike and Di. There've been so few young people at The Camp this summer. Last summer there were the Whitleys and the two Richardson boys; but the Richardsons have been traveling in Europe this year, and I'm not sure just where the Whitleys have been. So your presence has been much appreciated, I'm sure." She exhaled a large cloud of smoke and regarded James thoughtfully through half-closed eyes. "I hear the Richardsons are back now and are due to arrive at The Camp any day. That will be nice, won't it? You'll like Lance and Gary, I'm sure. Mike and Di are very fond of them."

"Hey, I'm sorry." James got to his feet as Diane

ran down the stairs. "That Barbie. She's incredible. I've been listening this whole time. She wouldn't let me talk long enough to even tell her I had company. I tried and —watch out, James!"

Whirling, James stumbled over the lion's head and lurched to one side as Jacky's golf ball missed him by inches and crashed into a lampshade. The lamp rocked and righted itself while Jacky chased after the ball, and Mrs. Jarrett chased after Jacky. When she caught him, she explained to him that it was very bad of him to throw his ball at people and that the only reason he did it was because he was hungry and tired and needed his lunch and a nap. And she was going to take him upstairs, and Ethel would make him something nice to eat. After James and Diane watched Mrs. Jarrett carry Jacky up the stairs, they went out and sat on the deck and talked about swimming and parental hang-ups and other more personal topics.

James asked about the swimming meet, and Diane said it had been a bore. "I used to really be into the whole swimming thing," she said. "I used to work out three hours every day, and I really got off on going to the meets and winning awards and having my picture in the papers and all that power trip. But then when I began to get more interested in other things, I got sick of having to spend so much time in the water. So I switched over to diving because it's not so much a matter of stamina and I can be very good at it without spending nearly so much time practicing. In fact, my coach is always telling me that if I'd work even half as hard as other divers I could probably be an Olympic champion. But I'm getting sick of the diving now, too. And this

9 5

Sacramento thing was really a bore. I only went to it because my father wanted me to, and I couldn't even get interested enough to really try." She reached over and put her hand on James' and then made her hand walk on two fingers—and somehow made the two fingers suggest the sexy way she had of walking—up his arm to his shoulder and then made it jump up and put one finger on his lips. "Besides," she said, looking at him out of the corners of her eyes, "I had other things on my mind. More exciting things."

He grabbed her hand and pulled her around, and they kissed quickly before she pulled away and glanced back at the picture window. "We'd better watch it," she said. "My mother."

"Is she pretty puritanical?" James asked.

"Puritanical? Oh you mean anti-sex? No, not particularly. I mean she laughs at dirty jokes and goes to X-rated movies and things like that. But there are some things that really drive her up the wall. Like Dad's girlie magazines—and *anything* I do. Anything at all about me. I think the thing is, she hasn't realized I'm not ten years old anymore. And my dad is just as bad, only in a different way."

"In a different way?" James asked. And she started telling him about how her dad had always pushed her and Mike, too, to be the best at everything and take part in all kinds of competitions and win prizes and awards and trophies, and how it was obvious that what mattered to him was winning, even though he kept saying that what really mattered was giving it all you had. While she was talking, James watched her and nodded and made appropriate comments, and after a while she stopped talking and just stared at him. Then she smiled very seductively and made a kissing mouth and said, "Jamesy. You know something? I really like you. You know what I really like about you? The way you listen. A lot of people, and boys especially, just never want to listen to me at all. Most boys want to talk all the time themselves or"—she raised her eyebrows—"do other things. But you are a very good listener."

"Well thanks," James said. "Now that I come to think about it, it probably is one of my more creative talents." But what he was thinking was that if the truth were told, and it wasn't about to be, he hadn't been listening all that carefully. What he'd been doing, along with listening just enough to make a comment now and then, was thinking about getting Diane to walk down to the road with him when he left and wondering if she would agree to a detour into the woods, again, on the way.

Not long afterwards Mrs. Jarrett called Diane to come to lunch, but when he asked her to walk as far as the road with him, she agreed. On the way down the hill he asked when he could see her again, and she suggested that they meet at the lake the next morning and go swimming together. Since she had to hurry back to lunch, their detour into the trees was very brief, but very passionate. James was still breathing hard when they got to the end of the drive and, because of the picture window, said good-by very discreetly. He was just stepping out into the road when there was a sudden roar, and he jumped back as a silver-colored Porsche rounded the curve and swept past them. A hand waved above the roof on the driver's side, and someone yelled, "Hey, Di!"

"Lance!" Diane called. "Hi, Lance." She waved and went on waving until the car disappeared.

"Well, good-by again, until tomorrow," James said.

"Oh," she said. "Good-by. You know who that was? That was Lance Richardson—in a new car. The Richardsons are back."

"Yeah," James said. "Your mother mentioned them. Well, I'd better be on my way. Good-by, Diane, and—" Cocking both hands he gave her favorite salute. "Ka-pow!"

Diane's answering "Ka-pow," seemed slightly pre-occupied.

CHAPTER 8

IT WAS an old fantasy involving a gorgeous sexily dressed girl who practically pounced on him as he was walking innocently through a hotel lobby and by some transparent ruse or other got him to accompany her to her room where she immediately began to initiate a lot of wildly exciting activities—the kind of thing that apparently happened to Max quite frequently but that James, himself, had only read and fantasized about. The difference was that recently the fantasy girl had had a recognizable face. A sleek tan face with reckless gold-brown eyes and a kiss-shaped mouth.

He sighed and threw back his blanket so that only a sheet protected him from the fresh morning air. It seemed warmer than usual. He closed his eyes again and let himself sink back into reverie and once again conjured up her face. Diane was undoubtedly—and unexaggeratedly, in spite of what Max had implied in his last letter—the sexiest girl James had ever seen. Beside her, Trudi Hepplewhite faded into drab obscurity. He sighed again as the fantasy face rolled its beautiful eyes and curled its perfect lips in a familiar smile—a smile that simultaneously teased, challenged and invited.

"—and beyond appearance?"

Unexpected and unsolicited, the question appeared below the fantasy face like a subtitle in a foreign movie. But not out of the blue. It had been asked before—just the night before, in fact, by Charlotte, in the midst of a discussion concerning what James had been doing with his time lately. He had considered telling Charlotte before, and this time when she asked, he had suddenly said, "I've been falling in love."

"Oh, really? I somehow had a feeling something of the sort was involved. Tell me about her."

They had been sitting on the veranda at the time— just James and his mother—watching an enormous full moon float up over the eastern ridge of mountains, sending a golden trail across the black waters of the lake. The moonlight was bright enough for him to tell that she was looking at him with curiosity and with what seemed to be approval, which was just about the reaction he'd anticipated. Charlotte had always been very interested in emotions. When James was little, she was always asking him how he felt about things and telling him that it was important for people to stay in touch with their feelings. Once, when he'd asked her if his father was in touch with his feelings, she'd smiled in a funny way and said, "You know, I used to wonder about that, too. But then I discovered that your father has a perfectly normal quota of emotions. It's just that in his case they have a lot of intellectual activity to compete with. Actually, his emotions behave quite normally once you get their attention."

Having become accustomed to discussions of that sort, James felt free to bring up all kinds of topics—topics some people might consider unsuitable where parents were concerned. For instance, he'd mentioned more than once his feeling of inadequacy with girls and Charlotte had listened without making any of the useless comments you might expect from a person her age. Such as not to worry because it was only a phase he would be growing out of as he got older. She'd seemed to understand how frustrated he was about it, so he felt certain she'd be pleased to hear how things had changed since he'd met Diane.

He started at the beginning, telling her how they'd met and how easy Diane was to talk to. Apparently he'd also said a quite a lot about the way she looked because when he finally ran down, Charlotte had said, "—and beyond appearance?"

"What do you mean?" he asked.

"I just mean I'd like to know about her as a person. The kinds of things she's interested in—likes—dislikes, the things you have in common, perhaps."

So he'd mentioned that Diane played tennis and a little about her swimming and diving. He didn't go into the hunting thing, knowing how Charlotte felt about the subject. Then he'd thought for a while and added, "And another thing we have in common is"—he paused and grinned to make clear that he wasn't entirely serious —"Me!" Charlotte's reaction made him feel that it wasn't necessary to explain any further—to go into what a surprise it had been to find that someone like Diane was interested in him. He didn't go into the chemistry thing either—about how he reacted physically to Diane and how she apparently reacted to him.

Shifting over onto his back, he put his arm behind his head and went on thinking about the things he and Diane had in common. After a while he decided it didn't really matter, anyway. That is, it didn't mean that they couldn't have a significant and important relationship. Look at all the love affairs in literature where the lovers had very little in common. After some thought he came up with Phillip and Mildred in *Of Human Bondage* and David Copperfield and Dora, which might not have been what you'd call ideal matches, but certainly would have to be called significant. And besides, there was lots of time in which they might develop interests in common. Something might start developing at any time—a thought that led to the time at the moment—and the fact that he had an eleven o'clock date to meet Diane at the lake.

He reached the spot they agreed on, a stretch of lakeshore near the first boathouse, a little early and stretched out to work on his tan while he waited. The breeze was cool, but the clean, sharp warmth of the mountain sun tingled the skin of his back and legs. The air smelled damply of sand and lake, spiced now and then by breezes laden with the sun-warmed scent of pine and fir. All of it, the smells, the sensuous comfort of sun and sand, the anticipation of Diane's arrival, blended into a strangely vivid feeling of timelessness, a sense that this moment was everlasting, would go on existing, returning again and again, like sunrise or the first day of spring. The shining moment dimmed and lengthened, drifted into semi-conciousness and then back into an awareness of a numb arm and a back that was a little too warm for comfort. He sat up and looked at his watch. It was almost twelve o'clock.

When he dialed the Jarrett's number from the snack bar phone booth, Diane answered the phone. "Oh hi," she said. "Wait a minute. I'm going to another phone." There was a slight thump and then nothing except the distant sound of several people talking and laughing. Then someone shouted, No, Jacky. Don't—" a click and the line was dead.

James stared into the earpiece. "I don't believe it," he said. Fishing in the pocket of his trunks, he discovered he was out of dimes. After Fiona had torn herself away from a conversation with a muscle-bound guy in green coveralls who was restocking the ice cream freezer, she finally changed his quarter and he got back to the phone booth. This time the phone rang quite a while before Diane answered it.

"Hi Jamesy," she said. "I'm sorry. Jacky hung up on us."

"So I gathered. I just called to ask if you were coming to the lake, like we planned."

"The lake? Oh, did we say we'd meet there for sure? I thought you just said you'd call to see if I could come down."

He decided against saying how sure he was they'd made it definite. "Well. I'm calling," he said instead. "Are you coming down?"

There was a long pause. "I'm afraid I can't right now. We have company. Friends of the family. My mother wouldn't want me to leave right now."

There was a silence while James tried to deal with his anger.

"I'm sorry, Jamesy," Diane said. Her voice was soft, seductive, pleading. "Don't be mad at me. Maybe we can go swimming tomorrow. Okay?"

He said he wasn't mad at her. When the conversation was over, he went on sitting in the phone booth for several minutes, glumly considering the possibilities for the rest of the day. He would just as soon have gone on home, except that he had told Charlotte about his date to go swimming with Diane and he didn't feel like going into explanations right at the moment. Finally he decided rather bitterly to go back to the beach and, in the interest of symmetry, sunburn his stomach to match his back. After ordering an egg sandwich at the sidewalk window, he trudged back across the sand.

The egg salad sandwich turned out to be made of a little lettuce and a lot of goopy mayonnaise and a few small lumps that you could believe were hard-boiled egg, if you felt optimistic, but which in his present state of mind he was inclined to view with suspicion. Closing his eyes and making a determined effort to think positively, he finished the sandwich and collapsed in the sand. The air had lost its cool tingle, and the sand felt hot and itchy. Eyes closed tightly and teeth clenched, he had been determinedly tanning for about ten minutes when someone said, "Hello Prince." Sitting up, he looked quickly around. There was no one on the beach except himself.

"Hello," the voice said again, and following the sound, he looked up at the dock of the nearest boathouse. Griffin Donahue was leaning over the rail looking down at him. Her long braid of sunstreaked hair, dangling two feet below her face, looked almost as wide as her neck, and tight-fitting blue jeans accentuated the narrow length of her body. Seen from below, her wide long-eyed face looked vaguely oriental.

"Oh it's you," he said. "What are you doing up there?"

"Feeding things."

"Yeah? What kind of things?" He grinned, raising his eyebrows in mock apprehension. "Or should I ask?"

She didn't smile. "Do you want to see?" she asked.

"Sure. Why not?"

The dock was well posted with *Keep Off* and *Private Property* signs, and a padlocked chain blocked access by unauthorized vehicles. As he stepped over the chain, James noticed the wooden sign that hung from it. The name *Westmoreland* was carved into the wood in artistically rustic script, and the boathouse itself, one of the largest on the lake, followed The Camp's architectural guidelines—a style that James had recently, in a letter to Max, dubbed "Ghost Town Lavish." He followed Griffin past the crossbarred double doors of the main entrance and around to the side of the building. At a small side entrance she stopped and took a key from her pocket. Picking up a paper bag, which had been sitting near the door, she looked back at James and said, "Shh. Come in very quietly."

The light was dim. Just below floor level a large cabin-type motor boat rocked gently, its polished chrome and shiny enamel reflecting the soft light. At dock level a narrow strip of walkway ran around three sides of the boathouse and a block and tackle arrangement dangled from the ceiling beams. Near the double doors a spiral wrought iron stairway led to an upper floor. Griffin closed the small door behind them very softly, and the light became even dimmer.

"Shh," she said again. Motioning for James to follow her, she led the way to a coil of rope near the outer edge of the walkway. "Sit down," she whispered. She waited until he was seated on the rope and then knelt and crawled to where a flight of steps led down to the deck of the boat. Leaning forward, she rapped sharply with her knuckles on the top stair.

James found himself staring with unblinking fascination, expecting—almost anything. His eyes still weren't completely adjusted to the dim light, and now, as Griffin leaned into the flickering light reflecting up from the rippling water, the outlines of her bent back and reaching arms wavered and swam, transforming themselves into slender swaying patterns. He was still staring when a scrabbling noise caught his attention, and following the sound, he looked down in time to see a small black hand appear on the edge of the second stair. He caught his breath in an involuntary gasp of astonishment. The hand disappeared.

Griffin looked back, frowning, and her lips noiselessly formed a "shh." Then she rapped on the step again. The black hand reappeared, followed by a second one and then a long slender black nose. A small masked face twisted to look up at her, and then a raccoon crawled out onto the step from a narrow space between the dock and the boathouse floor. Whispering something under her breath, she pulled the paper bag slowly towards her and took out a handful of kibbled dog food. As she slowly extended her hand, the raccoon raised a handlike paw and took a few morsels from her palm.

When it had eaten the first mouthful, Griffin moved back and he followed, climbing up onto the floor of the boathouse. A moment later a second raccoon appeared on the stair, and then a third.

They were aware of James. Their dainty black noses twitched in his direction and their eyes and ears scanned him anxiously from time to time; but then returning to Griffin, they seemed to dismiss him as something of hers; as something potentially dangerous but made safe and acceptable by her presence. Crouching on the coil of rope, James watched in almost breathless fascination as Griffin went on feeding and talking to the animals. He couldn't hear what she was saying. In fact, at times it hardly seemed to be words at all; but her lips moved, and he could make out a soft stream of sound. The raccoons circled in front of her, small furry hunchbacked shapes, bobbing their heads and making soft growling noises. One at a time they came closer, squatted on their haunches, held out both hands, or reached out to touch her bent knees. As each one approached, she seemed to speak to it individually, and each of them responded, looking up at her face and making the soft, throaty noises. When she held out handfuls of kibble, they sat up and reached for it with both hands, scooping it up gently between their palms. When the food was gone, they went on weaving and bobbing around her, touching her feet and legs, exploring the empty bag, scurrying away when their explorations brought them too close to where James was sitting. After a long time she stood up, and as if at a signal, the raccoons filed down the stairs and disappeared beneath the flooring. Back in the bright sunlight on the dock, the spell faded slowly. Griffin seemed distant, almost distracted. Walking beside her, James watched her curiously.

After a while he asked, "How did you tame them?"

"Tame them?" Her eyebrows, oddly dark and heavy in contrast to her blue eyes and sun-streaked hair, drew together in a thoughtful frown. "I didn't. Not really. I just saw one of them one day, and so I sat down and talked to him until he wasn't afraid anymore. And then the others came. They just aren't very afraid of me."

"I know. It's amazing."

She shrugged. "Most animals are very intelligent. They know if you're their friend."

That was what reminded him of the deer and of his promise to take her to see him—a promise he regretted making and hoped she'd forgotten. But now, as if reading his mind, she said, "When are you going to take me to see . . ."

She paused, staring up at him, and almost as if there was something hypnotic about her high-intensity blue eyes, he found himself saying, ". . . to see the deer?"

She nodded. "The deer," she said.

"Well, how about right now," he said, to his own amazement. "I don't seem to have much else to do this afternoon." Even while he was saying it, he was telling himself he was crazy. To give away his most treasured secret, a secret he hadn't shared with anyone, to a crazy little kid he really knew very little about. Perhaps she really did have some mysterious power of persuasion. Or, more likely, he just wanted some company, any company, to keep from brooding over the fact that

Diane had stood him up. And on the positive side, there was no doubt that Griffin loved animals and would never intentionally do anything to endanger the deer.

They had already started up Anzio when he realized that Griffin's feet, bare as usual, presented a problem. Her feet were probably pretty well toughened, but there were some stretches of very rough terrain on the way to the valley. When he mentioned the need for shoes, she didn't argue.

"When we go past my house, I'll run in and get some," she said.

"All right. But that presents another problem. If Woody sees you, he'll want to come along and I wouldn't want to take a kid that young over the cliff trail. There are some places where it's pretty dangerous."

She shook her head. "Woody's not at home. He's gone to Belvedere with Wes."

"Wes?"

"Yes. His father. They're visiting Woody's grandparents. The Westmoreland ones. And they're going to a specialist to see why he gets tonsillitis so much. They'll be back in a couple of days."

"Did they leave you all alone?"

"Oh no. My mother is here and a whole lot of other people. It's a kind of party."

A few minutes later he saw what she meant. As the Westmoreland's house came into view, he saw that several cars were parked along the road, and five or six more in the parking area beside the house. And if the cars were any indication, the guests weren't little old ladies from Pasadena. Near the driveway James stopped to stare in appreciation at a fantastic Jaguar and a brand new Ferrari. Party noises, music, loud voices, laughter, drifted down to Anzio, and looking up, James saw a lot of people sitting around small tables on the lower deck.

"I'll just go up and get my shoes," Griffin said. "Do you want to wait here?"

It was obvious that that was what she wanted him to do. "I might as well," he said. "I wouldn't want to intrude at lunchtime."

She shook her head. "Breakfast," she said. "I'll just be a minute." She had started up the slope when a man and a woman came out into the parking area, followed by what looked, from a distance, to be a pack of long-legged rats. A moment later a flashy looking silver-brown sports car roared into life, shot backwards, and then swooped down the drive. Beside Griffin it slid to a stop, and the window on the passenger side opened.

Sun on the windshield made it hard for James to see the woman clearly, but it was obvious that the conversation was, at least in part, about him. Several times Griffin gestured in his direction. The woman was probably her mother, and under the circumstances, it seemed diplomatic to go up and be introduced. If Mrs. Westmoreland was objecting to her thirteen-year-old daughter going off on a hike with an older guy, and it seemed quite likely that she was, he felt fairly certain he could set her mind at ease. And he might as well do it. Being the type who wouldn't ever be mistaken for Mack the Knife wasn't always an asset; so when it was, it might as well be taken advantage of. He strode resolutely up the drive, smiling his most forthright and reliable smile.

On closer inspection, the car was a Maserati, and

the woman in the passenger seat was the most incredible-looking person he'd ever seen. A general description might include such things as shadowy blue eyes, lots of tawny hair, deeply tanned skin, a silky white jumpsuit with a belt of golden chains and the body to go with it. In spite of her coloring, she gave an impression of dark-ness—a subtle brooding darkness, exotic and foreign. But no listing of details would explain the overall effect that was a kind of dazzle, like fireworks in a black sky. Who-ever she was—film star, international beauty, sex god-dess—she obviously wasn't Griffin's mother.

"This is my mother," Griffin was saying.

He swallowed twice before he managed to get started explaining the little educational nature hike he and Griffin were planning. He got in most of the infor-mation he wanted to cover, but the delivery was lousy, accompanied by a lot of blinking and stammering. As he blundered along, Mrs. Westmoreland watched him with a disconcerting lack of concern. His explanation seemed to be working—if not in quite the way he'd intended. He would have preferred to have given the impression of being reassuringly responsible, rather than harmlessly imbecilic. As he babbled, the woman's eyes drifted dreamily from his face down to her lap, where three skinny little dogs whimpered and shivered. After a while he began to get the feeling that she wasn't listen-ing to him. Before he was quite through, she sighed, smiled sleepily and reached out to touch Griffin's cheek with the backs of her fingers.

"That's nice, darlings," she said. "Don't get lost." The man at the wheel, whom James had forgotten to even notice, shot the car into gear, and it roared down the drive.

"Wow," James said. "That's really your mother?"

But Griffin was already running at top speed toward the house.

CHAPTER 9

GRIFFIN's eyes were firmly fixed on her feet—now encased in scruffy tennis shoes—and her responses to all of James' conversational efforts were as brief as possible. When he asked if the party was to celebrate anything in particular, and who the man in the car with her mother was, she simply shrugged and said she didn't know. And when he said her mother was fantastically good-looking, her answer was even briefer. "I know," she said in a flat voice. He was beginning to wonder if he'd doomed himself to a hike that would turn out to be not only ill-advised but also embarrassingly silent. But just before they reached the west gate he hit on a subject that produced better results. When he asked about the dogs, she said they were whippets; and although she was still looking at her feet, her voice definitely had more life in it. He decided to try a variation on the same theme.

"Was something wrong with them? They seemed to be shivering?"

"No. Nothing's wrong with them. They're just

very nervous. And they don't like strangers. They're very sensitive."

"They're bred for racing aren't they? Does your mother race them?"

"No. Wes has some that he races, but they live at the trainer's. My mother just has hers for pets. She takes them with her everywhere."

With a little more encouragement, Griffin went on talking about the dogs for quite a while—their names, their personalities and how intelligent they were. Obviously her rapport with wild animals extended to dogs as well.

"Do you have a dog of your own?" James asked.

"No. I can't because I go to a boarding school and they don't allow dogs, but Woody and I get to take care of the whippets when my mother's at home. When she goes away, she usually takes them with her."

"Was she going away just now?" It didn't seem likely that a person would take off in the midst of their own party, but he was beginning to get the feeling that Alexandra Griffith Westmoreland's behavior wouldn't necessarily follow any pattern with which he was familiar.

"No." She was looking at her shoes again. "She said they were just going down to the Commissary for things they needed for breakfast. Bacon and gin and things like that."

"Gin—for breakfast?"

"Gin fizzes?" Her tone implied that gin fizzes were at least as much a breakfast necessity as bacon, if not more so.

"Oh sure," he said. "Gin fizzes."

When they reached the Willowby trail, he turned up it, explaining to Griffin that he had to change his clothes and get some apples for the deer. Griffin said she'd wait there.

"You might as well come along. You can wait for me on the porch. My parents are working. You won't have to meet them unless you want to."

She nodded, but she stayed where she was until he was almost out of sight, then yelled, "Okay. I'm coming," and ran after him. When they got within sight of the Willowby cabin, she froze again; but this time when he turned back, he saw that she was staring like a kid getting a first glimpse of Disneyland.

The Willowby cabin was one of the earliest buildings in the entire area, according to Dan Willowby whose grandfather started building it way back when the only access to the area was by mule train. The part he'd built then, one large room of rough logs, was now used as the living room, and over the years several other additions had been tacked on at various angles and elevations. The general effect was what might be called picturesque, if you liked that sort of thing, or ramshackle, if you didn't.

As far as James' personal feelings went, he could appreciate the cabin's long history and the irregular, slightly saggy appearance that made it seem more like a natural happening than the result of any intentional construction effort. There were, however, some bits of rustic authenticity that he'd be glad to do without—such as the untrustworthy toilet and the propane stove that seemed determined to self-destruct. But, generally speaking, he could relate, at least to some extent, to Griffin's enthusiasm.

"It's a real cabin," she said in an awestruck voice. "And *old*. It's really very old, isn't it?" Brushing past him she climbed the steps to the lopsided veranda very slowly, looking around at the rough wooden shutters and rusty lounge swing as if they were part of a museum exhibit of artifacts from some ancient civilization. "Real logs," she said, running her fingers along the wall; and when James said, "Full of real dry rot," she only nodded and there was something so eager and unguarded about her face that he felt a little guilty for wising off. He left her still exploring as enthusiastically as if she were visiting one of England's stately homes; and when he came back a few minutes later, dressed for hiking, he found her in the midst of a conversation with Charlotte.

He heard their voices when he was crossing the living room, and it really surprised him because when he went in, Charlotte had been in the study at the other end of the house typing away on William's manuscript. But now, suddenly, there she was sitting on the swing beside Griffin, rapping as if they were old friends.

"There you are, James," she said. "Griffin and I have been discussing Willowby history and some of those old houses on Marshall Street in New Moon. She's actually been inside that one with the funny little tower."

"It belongs to an old woman I met at the library," Griffin said. "When I told her I liked old houses, she took me through it."

"Would you like to see the cabin before you go?" Charlotte asked.

James could see that there wasn't much point in protesting, so he only mentioned that they needed to get started and sat down on the veranda railing to wait. Fifteen minutes later they came back, still talking.

"We've got to get started," he told his mother. "We're going on a pretty long hike."

"Yes," she said. "Griffin was just telling me."

He nodded, wondering just how much Griffin had told her.

"Will you be gone long?"

"Most of the afternoon. It's quite a long way."

Charlotte looked from James to Griffin and back again. He could see she was curious. He hoped she wasn't going to ask too many questions. "Well, be careful," she said. "And have a good time."

It soon became obvious that Griffin was as curious about Charlotte as Charlotte had been about her. On the way down to the lake she asked several questions about both of his parents—about the work they were doing and if they did the same kind of work when they were at home, and finally, if Charlotte was his real mother.

He grinned. "Well, as far as I know. My memories of our first meeting are a bit vague, but the rumor is it took place in the delivery room in the local hospital. Why do you ask?"

"I just wondered," was all she said.

"Wait a minute. I get it. It's the prince thing, isn't it? You're wondering if I was spirited away from the palace by my faithful nurse, Charlotte, to save me from the clutches of my evil Uncle Richard—or was it Boris?"

She didn't laugh. "No," she said. "I just wondered, because they're so different." She was beginning to act strange again, almost angry, so he dropped the subject and so did she.

When they got into the rugged terrain at the north end of the lake, she began to be hard to keep track of—in more ways than one. For one thing, keeping up a conversation with Griffin was enough to give you the intellectual bends. One moment she'd be chattering away about animals or one of the let's pretend games she played with Laurel and Woody, and the next she'd start discussing nuclear energy, or biofeedback, or the writings of Tolstoy.

In the midst of the steep zigzag climb to the first plateau, James was called upon to remember the end of *War and Peace*—it seemed the copy Griffin had inherited from the library was missing the last hundred, or so, pages. And somewhere among the boulders of the river-bed, he was asked if he thought biofeedback techniques could be used to cure alcoholism. When he got through giving his not-too-expert opinion on that one, he turned around to ask why she wanted to know and found she'd disappeared.

That was the other way she was hard to keep track of—physically. She kept turning up missing. Usually he found her exploring some interesting crevice in the rocks or following the tracks of an animal, but at the riverbed she was crouched behind a boulder with her hands covering her face. She didn't offer to explain, and he didn't ask.

When they had almost reached the beginning of

the cliff trail, he started wondering again if he'd made a terrible mistake. It was probably going to be a real problem getting Griffin over into the valley. The first time he crossed, he'd had moments of real panic when he was sure he couldn't go on and was even more certain he'd never get back the way he'd come. But when he started up the cliff, she stayed right behind him. When they reached the high ledge, he stopped and pointed out the rock by the deep pool directly below, where he'd first seen her—conducting the disenchantment of Prince Poisson.

"You really were watching—all the time?" She seemed a little embarrassed, but more pleased then anything else, and not at all bothered by the fact that he'd just knocked some large holes in the whole Prince Poisson story. He was sure she'd never admitted to anyone that it was all a fish story—in more ways than one. But then, since she was clearly capable of accepting him as both a long-term member of the Fielding household and a recently disenchanted fish, she probably had no trouble with his being simultaneously watching from the ledge and swimming around in the pool below. It was the kind of mind-boggling concept that made him feel slightly disoriented, and which, on a two-foot ledge over a perpendicular drop, seemed almost dangerously unbalanced.

"Come on," he said. "We'd better go. This next stretch is the trickiest part of the trail." He'd hardly started explaining the difficulties involved in negotiating the shale slide when she launched herself down it. She was waiting for him when he slid to a stop at the bottom.

He'd almost forgotten how incredible the valley was. He'd been amazed and excited when he first discovered it, but after having been there so many times, its impact had gradually faded. But now, watching Griffin, it was like seeing it again for the first time. On each side almost sheer rock walls streaked by strata and slanting rays of sunlight towered over the series of small meadows. And on the lush green grass of the first clearing, large outcroppings of bulbous black rock crouched like an invasion of gigantic black toads.

"That first boulder," he told Griffin, "the flattest one, is my usual observation post. Sometimes the stag comes—"

"The stag?"

He grinned self-consciously. "The deer," he said, "or buck. I just started calling him that sometimes. You know, the noble stag."

She nodded. "The noble stag," she whispered.

"Sometimes he comes right out onto the meadow while I'm sitting here," he went on. "But in the middle of the day he's usually lying down back in the woods near the spring. If he doesn't come out pretty soon, we'll go up there and look for him."

They sat on the boulder, Griffin hugging her knees up against her chest. She'd gone silent again, but her face was not the same as it had been during those other silences. She seemed to be completely unaware that he was watching her. Her eyes looked dilated and she breathed deeply, her lips slightly parted. After a while he began to feel a little nervous and he leaned closer forcing her to meet his eyes. She started, smiled vaguely and turned away.

They were still sitting there silently on the boulder when the deer came out of the pine grove. One moment there was only the green wall of pine and fir, and then suddenly there he was, standing in the slanting sunlight at the edge of the clearing. Griffin gasped and grabbed James' arm.

As many times as he'd seen him appear like that, it took James a minute before he could trust his voice. When he could, he said calmly, "Well, there he is. What do you think of him?"

"Shh," she breathed.

"It's all right. He's used to me talking to him. Watch." He slid slowly down off the boulder carrying the bag of apples. Moving slowly and continuing to talk in a low, soothing voice, he walked, not directly toward the deer, but obliquely out into the middle of the meadow. He left two apples near the center and then, retracing his steps, left two more quite close to the boulder. He had hardly climbed back up beside Griffin when the deer began to move forward. When he had finished the first two apples, he sniffed the air, staring at James and Griffin, and then tossed his head imperiously, as if he were protesting the necessity of subjecting himself to such close contact in order to receive their offerings.

"I think he's saying he'd rather be worshipped from afar," James said. Griffin only nodded. Her eyes transmitted excitement and now and then she pressed her knuckles against her mouth as if she were trying to keep her lips from trembling.

The deer relented then and moved closer, to the last two apples, and James forgot about Griffin in his own excitement at seeing him so much closer than ever before. He was noticing details—the smooth sleekness of the gray-brown coat, the patch of white on the wide chest, and the frayed areas on the antlers where the suedelike velvet was beginning to wear away, exposing smooth dark horn. When the apples were gone, he retreated several yards and then stopped to test the air again, perhaps trying to determine if there were more apples, or checking out the new person who had invaded his domain. With his curiosity apparently satisfied, he turned at last and paced majestically into the deep shadows of the grove.

Griffin went on sitting absolutely still, her chin resting on her knees, her eyes riveted on the spot where the deer had disappeared.

James waited. "Well what do you think?" he said at last. For another moment there was no response, and when it came, it was only a quick turn and a brief smile like a sudden flash of light, and then she was gone again, back into some private world of her own. After a while he tried again. "It's getting late. We'd better get started or we'll be late to dinner. At least I will." There was no telling when dinner happened in a household that had gin fizz breakfasts at one o'clock in the afternoon. After another longish period she nodded slowly and slid down off the rock.

That was the way it was all the way home. Just as at the beginning of the hike, Griffin had become almost completely nonverbal. It was a different kind of silence, but the end result was the same: a lack of communication that got to be almost embarrassing after a while. Taken as a whole, the entire day had turned out to be fairly uncomfortable, and, of course, he had no one to blame but himself. It served him right for giving in to a sudden impulse to share something that had been his own and private with a kooky kid, just because it had seemed like a good thing to do at the moment. It had been a dumb move, and it might very well turn out to be a lot more serious than a wasted day. How did he know, for instance, that she wouldn't start shooting off her mouth about the deer to everyone she knew.

When they finally reached the spot where the path to the west gate branched off, he said. "Look. It's late. I think I'll just go on home if you don't mind going on alone."

It took a minute to get through, even then, but at last she said, "Oh no, I don't mind."

"There's one thing though. I just want to remind you not to tell anyone about the valley. I mean, the deer's life depends on it. I've found out enough about trophy hunting lately to know that he's really one in a million—as a trophy. And if word got out, every hunter in the whole country would be up here gunning for him the minute hunting season starts."

He finally had her full attention. She was staring at him as if he'd just started growing a second head. "As a trophy!" She seemed to be having trouble getting the words out.

"Yes. You know. A stuffed head."

She nodded fiercely. "I know. Like all those things in the Jarretts' house."

That jolted him, for some reason—probably because of his relationship with Diane. He found himself feeling a little defensive. "Well, yes. I guess the thing is, they go by the number of points and the width and symmetry of the horns, and this deer must be really unusual. I think it's because he's managed to live a lot longer than most bucks do nowadays, by holing up in that valley during hunting season. So if people start finding out about the valley," he made a neck chopping motion, "it's curtains."

Griffin actually shuddered. She narrowed her eyes and between her heavy lashes they seemed almost to smoke with intensity. "I would never tell any of those people about the stag," she said. "Never! They're murderers."

"Well!" James grinned. "I don't know about that. They're hunters. That's not quite the same thing."

"They're murderers," she insisted. "They look like murderers. Their names even sound like it. Hank and Jill—yank and kill."

He couldn't help laughing. "How about Jack-whack."

"And Mike-strike," she said.

"How about Diane?" he asked, thinking there was nothing very fierce sounding about a name like Diane.

"They call her Di, don't they?" Griffin said.

He hadn't thought of that, or he wouldn't have mentioned it. "Well, okay," he said. "I didn't really think you would tell anyone, but I just thought I'd mention it."

He was turning to leave when she grabbed his arm. "Thank you," she said. "Thank you, thank you, thank you." Then she whirled away and began to run.

When James got back to the cabin, he discovered that Charlotte had jumped to a ridiculous conclusion. "That girl?" he said. "No." He was in the midst of pulling off a boot at the time, and he almost tipped over laughing. "No. That's Griffin. She told you her name was Griffin."

"But that's not a name," Charlotte said. "It's some kind of heraldic beast, isn't it? I thought perhaps it was a nickname or a joke of some sort. And after hearing all about Diane just the other night, it never occurred to me you were interested in another girl as well."

"Interested?" He stared at his mother in disbelief. "In that little kid?"

"Dear me." Charlotte looked chagrined. "I'm really embarrassed to have made such an incredible error. How old is this—child, anyway?"

"Oh, I don't know. About thirteen, I think."

"Ah. I see."

He caught the twitch of lips that obviously meant Charlotte thought thirteen wasn't all that much younger than almost sixteen. "Okay," he grinned. "So thirteen isn't exactly another generation, but there is a big difference. If you saw Diane, you'd know what I'm talking about."

"Yes, I'm sure I would." Charlotte said. "But who is this Griffin, then?"

"Just a kid who happens to be very interested in wildlife and things like that. I promised to take her to see a place I discovered where you can usually see some interesting things. Oh, and about her name—she's called Griffin because her real name is Griffith, which is pretty strange, too, especially for a girl. Her mother is that woman we were talking about the other day. That Alexandra Griffith, whose name is Westmoreland now."

"Oh," Charlotte said. "Well, of course. I knew she

made me think of someone. She does look quite remarkably like her mother, doesn't she? When her picture was always in the papers, I remember thinking that, as much as I disapproved of her antics, she really was quite fantastically beautiful. I take it you've met her—Alexandra Griffith?"

"Yes. I just did today. And I guess they do look something alike, now that you mention it." It really hadn't occurred to him before. "The thing is, everything else about them seems to be so different. I didn't even notice about the appearance thing."

"I see," Charlotte said.

CHAPTER 10

I'M AWFULLY SORRY about yesterday, Jamesy." Diane took hold of his hand and squeezed it hard. He squeezed back and pulled her to a stop. They had been walking across the patio towards the Jarretts' kitchen door, and now when James bent to kiss her, she rolled her eyes towards the house. The top half of the Dutch door was open, and from inside the sound of women's voices drifted out into the patio.

"It's my mother and aunt," she whispered, "having their daily gossip session. You know—who's not invited to whose party, who's hitting on whose wife, who ought to join Weight Watchers—that sort of thing."

"Let's not go in," James said.

"Oh, come on. I'm thirsty. Then we can go on down to the trophy room and be—" she rolled her eyes "—alone."

In the kitchen, Jill Jarrett and another woman were sitting at the breakfast bar drinking coffee. Angela Jarrett was smaller and darker than her sister-in-law, but there seemed to be a similarity about them. It wasn't so much in their actual features, as in their clothing and mannerisms and the sound of their voices. They both said hello with an exceptional amount of warmth and enthusiasm, and then immediately turned their backs and went on with their conversation. Diane was busy rummaging around in the refrigerator.

"It's not the little boy that worries me," Angela was saying. "It's that older child—Griffin, they call her. Laurel seems to absolutely idolize her. She'd spend every waking hour with the two of them if I'd let her. I've been trying to discourage it, and Dunc agrees with me, for once. He thinks there's something very strange about both of them."

"With good reason," Jill Jarrett said. "Coming from that background."

"Well, as far as family background goes, you couldn't do much better than the Griffiths, or the West-morelands for that matter. But I know what you mean. The Alexandra thing."

"Ethel says they both drink like fishes, and that the children are allowed to run wild. Apparently they do have them in very good schools during the year, but here at The Camp they just allow them to run wild in the woods day after day."

"Considering what goes on at some of those mara-thon parties, the woods might be the safest place for them. You know the Arthurs were asked once, and afterwards Caroline told me . . ." Angela glanced over her shoulder and lowered her voice.

"Would you like Pepsi or apple cider?" Diane stuck a couple of cold bottles in James' hands and led the way out of the room. He followed, but the kitchen conversation, and some questions it brought up, were still on his mind. All the way down the stairs and across the dozen or so yards of trophy room to the leather couch by the coffee table, he mulled over possible answers and implications.

"About the Westmorelands," he said when they were settled on the couch.

Tipping her head back against his shoulder, Diane took a long drink from her Pepsi before she answered. Leaving her head where it was, she said, "What about the Westmorelands?"

"About what your mother and aunt were saying in the kitchen . . ."

"Were they talking about the Westmorelands? I didn't notice. I get tired of their stories. Usually it's stuff I heard weeks ago. What were they saying about the saggy swingers."

"The saggy swingers?"

"The Westmorelands and all their swinging friends. That's what Lance and Gary call them, because most of them are really old, like way over thirty. And they're always having these wild parties. Some of them are just blasts, with booze and dope, but they go in for all the latest head trips, too. All kinds of touchy-feely encounter things like body awareness and—" she looked up at him and wiggled her eyebrows "—and group massage."

"Do your parents go to their parties?" he asked.

She laughed. "My parents? No. My mother says nothing could make her go to one of those parties, but I'll bet she'd go if she got a chance. Out of curiosity, for one thing. She's dying to find out about them. But the Westmorelands don't have much to do with most of the people here at The Camp. They never go to the Major's social things; and whenever they're here, they usually bring a lot of their jet-setty friends along with them."

"How'd you find out about the parties then?"

"Oh, everybody talks about them. They hire New Moon people to work at the parties sometimes. Ethel's cooked for them a couple of times; and Bertha, who cleans for us, works for them sometimes, too. My mom always pumps them about the Westmorelands. And everybody tries to pump Laurel, too—that's my little brat of a cousin—because she plays with the Westmoreland kids a lot.

"Do you know Griffin?"

"Is that the girl? Yes, I've met her. Laurel brought her here once. That was really a scene. She had a kind of fit and called my dad a murderer."

"A murderer?" James said. But his surprise only lasted a moment because then he got the picture. "Oh, you mean because of this room—the trophies?"

"Yes. It was really a scene. She's as nutty as they come."

He found himself feeling a little defensive about Griffin, which didn't make a whole lot of sense, since he'd often thought of her as a bit dippy himself. "It was probably just because she's so crazy about animals," he said. "She really has a thing about them. She probably just got upset about your father killing so many of them."

Diane shrugged. "Well, she's crazy. Because my dad probably likes animals just as much as she does. He really respects all the animals he hunts. He says hunting is kind of a game the hunter plays with the animals. A kind of matching wits thing." Diane was sitting up straight now, and her eyes looked angry. James decided not to ask whether the animals might prefer to play a game with slightly lower stakes. But he must have smiled a little because her eyes got angrier. "Besides," she said, "my dad says he's really doing them a favor when he shoots them, particularly the deer, because there are too many of them now because of all the predators being killed off, and if hunters didn't kill a lot of them every year, they'd just starve to death. And starving to death is a lot worse than being killed by a bullet." She was obviously getting pretty worked up, and when he reached for her hand she jerked it away.

"That makes sense," he said. "It really does. I hadn't thought about that before." He smiled a soothing smile and reached again for her hand. This time she allowed him to take it, but her lower lip, her beautiful moist lower lip, was still protruding a little bit more than usual. He was still thinking about the lip when she suddenly stood up.

"I'm getting extremely tired of this whole conversation," she said. "I think I'd like to go for a walk. Would you like to go for a walk with me, or would you rather go up and talk about your friend, Griffin, with my aunt and mother?"

James said he'd take the walk.

On the bottom deck, Jacky was bouncing up and down on a spring-mounted rocking horse. He had a particularly blank expression on his face, apparently lulled into an unnaturally peaceful state by the rhythmic rocking. He certainly seemed to have no aggressive thoughts on his mind and nothing in his hands except the horse's handlebars, but to be on the safe side, James did a quick check for bulging pockets before turning his back to go down the stairs. As he circled the horse, Jacky stopped bouncing and followed his progress, swiveling his head one way and then the other. "Hi there, Jacky," James said in a carefully unchallenging tone of voice. "What do you know?"

"Relax," Diane said. "There it is, under the window." She was pointing to where the golf ball was lying against the wall. "Besides, you don't have to worry any more. Dad made a deal with him. He's going to get a whole lot of toys and things if he doesn't throw the ball at people any more. Dad says Jacky is just like him. He's a tough customer, but when he makes a deal he sticks to it. Don't laugh. It's the truth. There've been lots of people around lately, and he hasn't thrown his ball at anyone. Have you, Jacky Whacky?"

She bent over Jacky and nuzzled his neck, but he only pushed her away and went on staring at James. Looking back, straight into the round brown eyes, James had a peculiar feeling that he was reading Jacky's mind. And if the message was what he thought it was, Diane's optimism might be a little premature. They went on down the stairs, and they were halfway down the driveway before Jacky stopped staring and went back to bouncing.

When they reached the end of the drive, James suggested they take their favorite trail into the nearest secluded grove of trees, but Diane said she was tired of always going to the same old place. She knew of another very private place to hike, she said, at the end of Bunker Hill.

"The end of Bunker Hill?" James said. "That's a long way." As far as he knew, the only way to get from Gettysburg to Bunker Hill was to go clear down to the Parade Grounds and then all the way up Bunker Hill. But Diane said she knew of a short cut, so they started off down Gettysburg.

Diane didn't seem to be in a very talkative mood. Remembering what she'd said about liking to be listened to, he made an effort to get her started talking. He tried several topics: books, movies, classes she liked best in school—or, all right then, hated least—and got very little response. But when he mentioned clothes, he got better results, particularly when he brought up the subject of tee shirt slogans. The one she was wearing said *Do Not Fold Staple or Mutilate*. When he said he liked it, she said it was a crummy old one. She had a new one she really liked but she hadn't finished fighting with her mother about it yet. About whether she was going to be allowed to wear it. It had a picture of Mt. Lassen on one side and Mt. Shasta on the other and underneath it said, *California's Most Perfect Peaks*. She was still telling who said what in the Perfect Peaks argument when they came to the shortcut to Bunker Hill.

The shortcut involved crossing a deep gully with a creek at the bottom. A very steep trail zigzagged through loose silty soil down to the bottom of the gully and the bed of the creek. The gully was private enough, but the steep dusty trail discouraged romantic pursuits, and the footing wasn't much better on the rocky creek bed.

But when he attempted to rise above such handicaps, Diane only twisted away from him, giggling, and started across the creek, jumping from stone to stone. But then, in midstream, she apparently changed her mind and held out her arms invitingly. He was beside her in one leap—and then began to slip backward. Diane squealed and ducked away from his clutching hands; and a moment later he was standing in knee-deep water, and she was climbing up the other side of the gully, laughing her head off.

The trail up the other side crossed what had obviously been a mudslide during the last rainy season and was now a deep drift of loose powdery silt. By the time James reached the top, his shoes and several inches of his denims were encased in a thick crust of mud and he was not in a very good frame of mind. His feet felt terrible and looked worse, and Diane wasn't helping matters by starting to giggle every time she looked at him. When they came out of the woods onto Bunker Hill, he stopped.

"I don't think I want to go any farther in this condition," he said. "I'll just head for home."

She stopped giggling immediately. "Don't go home," she said, putting her hand on his arm. "Please don't leave now. Just hike up to the end of Bunker Hill with me. Your shoes will dry and—" She glanced at his legs and her mouth twitched, but she kept it under control. "—and most of the mud will fall off when it gets drier. Please, go with me." James went.

Near the end of Bunker Hill they passed a cabin built along the lines of and roughly the same size as an airplane hangar. The doors of the triple garage were open and one of the cars inside was a silver Porsche.

"Wow! Who lives there?" James asked.

"Where?" Diane said, although there wasn't any other cabin in the vicinity. "Oh, there? That's the Richardsons' place."

For a moment it did occur to James to wonder if Diane's insistence on hiking up Bunker Hill was in any way related to the Richardsons, but as they walked past she didn't show any particular interest. In fact, just at that moment she began to show more interest in James than she had at any time since the hike started. Putting her arm around his waist, she leaned her head on his shoulder and began to talk about how tall he was and how much she liked tall men. He'd almost forgotten about the Richardsons when she suddenly said. "There's Mr. Richardson. Hi, Mr. Richardson! Hi, Stubby!"

A muscular-looking middle-aged man had appeared around the corner of the house, followed by a Doberman with a similar physique and a less friendly expression. Noticing James and Diane, the Doberman ran toward them barking, and the man ran after him calling his name. James had never had much confidence in Dobermans, and this one looked particularly untrustworthy. He was circling them with the hair bristling along the ridge of his back when Mr. Richardson caught up with him and grabbed him by the choke collar.

Diane introduced James and then asked Mr. Richardson how he was and how Mrs. Richardson was, and Lance and Gary. When Mr. Richardson had finished reporting on the health of the whole family, she asked how Stubby was, which seemed a bit unnecessary since there was obviously nothing wrong with his health, except that he was strangling himself in his eagerness to get at James.

Stubby's ominous interest in the calves of his legs had, at least, managed to take James' mind off his ridiculous-looking feet, until he noticed Richardson looking at them and grinning. "Looks like you've been covering some pretty rugged territory," he said.

Diane giggled. "He fell in the creek. Would it be all right if we used your hose to wash him off?"

Richardson told her to help herself, but James said, "Thanks a lot, but I don't think I'll bother. We'll have to go through all that loose dirt again on the way home, and they'll just get muddy again."

But Diane insisted. "Come on," she said. "We're going clear to the end of Bunker Hill first and they'll have plenty of time to dry. Grabbing James' hand she pulled him across the Richardsons' front yard. Mr. Richardson followed, and after he put Stubby in the house, he attached a hose to a faucet and Diane had just begun to spray James' feet when there was the sound of footsteps overhead. Someone was coming down the stairs from the front deck. "Hi, Lance," Diane called.

He looked to be about twenty or maybe even older, although Diane said later that he was eighteen. From the neck up he looked like an ad for the dry look, and from the neck down like something out of a show window on Rodeo Avenue in Beverly Hills—gold chains, designer jeans and high-heeled disco cowboy boots. Strolling towards them and then lounging against the wall of the house, he gave the impression that he couldn't get any more relaxed and stay conscious. When Diane introduced James, he turned his eyes, but not his whole head, in James' general direction and said, "Hey," and then to his father, "I'm taking the Targa into Tahoe. Okay?"

Mr. Richardson started asking questions and giving orders about not speeding and getting back before midnight, all of which obviously came close to boring his son into a complete coma. Yawning, he muttered, "Sure, sure," a couple of times, nodded at James and Diane and sauntered back around the corner. A few moments later the silver Porsche flowed down the driveway and disappeared down Bunker Hill.

When they'd said good-by and James had sloshed down the drive in his saturated shoes, Diane suddenly decided she didn't want to go to the end of Bunker Hill after all.

CHAPTER 11

WHEN he called Diane from the snack bar phone booth the day after the Bunker Hill hike, she said no, she couldn't come down and meet him. And when he asked if he could come up, she began to talk about how much she had to do and how she probably wouldn't have much time to talk to him even if he did.

"Okay," he said. "I'm beginning to get the picture. If you don't want to see me, why don't you just say so instead of throwing around a lot of unconvincing excuses."

"All right," she said. "I don't want to see you. At least not if you're going to talk to me like that. I don't like it when you scold me. If I want someone to scold me, I can always talk to my mother."

So then James said he hadn't realized his conversation was so unpleasant, and if she felt that way about it, perhaps he'd just better hang up. He waited for her to tell him not to, but she didn't, so he did. A minute later he was sorry, but it was too late.

That night he lay awake for hours thinking about

how it was all over and how he must have blown it somehow and wondering just what it was that he'd done wrong, and if Max would have been able to tell him, if he'd been there and seen it all.

It went on like that for three days and three nights. During the nights he stared into the darkness and thought about Diane, and during the days he sat at his desk and thought about her and tried to work on the da Vinci. Even though he was making a special effort to act normal around his parents, he must not have been entirely successful because he noticed Charlotte watching him closely, and once she even asked him if he wasn't feeling well.

James resented her curiosity. He wished she'd just leave him alone. It had nothing to do with her, and he didn't want anyone prying into his personal affairs and feeling sorry for him. Of course, William hadn't noticed anything. He wouldn't. His only son could have had delirium tremens, rabies and two broken legs and he probably wouldn't have noticed a thing. James resented his indifference.

On the morning of the fourth day he decided to go to the tennis courts. He didn't know why. He certainly didn't feel like playing tennis or anything else; and if Diane showed up and ignored him, it would only make things a million times worse. But somehow, once he'd thought of going, he couldn't seem to stop himself. He put on his favorite shirt, the bulky terry cloth one that tended to give his chest and upper arms a more muscular appearance, combed his hair very carefully and headed for The Camp.

He was sitting on the sidelines when she came in and

she saw him right away and waved her racket. His heart did a kind of lurch, but he stayed where he was, waiting to see what she would do. She stopped near the gate at first and looked around the court, and he was beginning to wonder, but then suddenly she whirled around and actually ran to meet him. For a moment he thought she was going to throw her arms around him right there in front of everyone. She didn't, but she was smiling her most devastating smile as she pointed the handle of her racket at him and said, "Ka-pow."

"Ka-pow," he said. "How are you?"

She made a kissing face. "Right at this moment I'm A-1, dynamite, primo. How about you?"

"More or less the same," he said.

Everything was right back the way it had been before, only better. For the next three days he saw Diane every day. They went swimming, played tennis and handball, sat around in the snack bar, or just hung out around the Parade Grounds together. Several times they went on short hikes into the woods. All of it was great, particularly the hikes, even though they were all very short.

The hikes, as James told Max, weren't primarily explorations of nature, unless you were referring to human nature. The only fauna involved was human, and the flora was only important because it provided privacy. And all forward progress tended to end at the first secluded spot on the trail. His letter to Max didn't go on to specify the other places at which his forward progress always ended. He wouldn't have told Max anyway, because it concerned Diane and was personal; but there was, he had to admit, another reason. Since most of the girls Max met seemed to have no set boundaries whatsoever, James wouldn't have been eager to tell him that Diane definitely did. Outside of those boundaries, she could be wildly, recklessly, maddeningly passionate, but at certain places everything came to a stop. James told Max it was all wildly, recklessly passionate, and let it go at that.

Every day seemed better and more exciting than the last, and the nights changed, too. Instead of lying awake brooding and sighing, he was now lying awake daydreaming and fantasizing. All of the fantasies were about Diane, and some of them weren't even sexy, at least not very. Nearly all of them were about the future and concerned things that might happen in the fall, or in the next five or ten years. One of the most vivid was about what it would be like to have Diane as a girl friend when the summer was over and they were both back in school. There would be visits back and forth—Sacramento wasn't all that far away; and perhaps if Charlotte got to know the Jarretts and offered to chaperone, Diane might even be allowed to stay for a weekend. The weekend visit fantasy always included the introduction of Diane to Max, and the comments he would make afterwards, and football games and dances to which James would take Diane and the sensation she would undoubtedly create.

Of course, he realized that such daydreams were on a par with that old favorite—"the triumphant return to the old home town"—and as such not only egotistical, but also juvenile and unoriginal. But at least he was aware of it, and capable of kidding himself about it. It was the kind of thing he intended to outgrow in the near future, but in the meantime it was a lot more fun than counting sheep.

There were other fantasies, too, that had to do with the future. Some distant, dimly seen future in which he and Diane would be living together in a tastefully funky apartment—old wicker furniture, huge floor pillows, Chagall prints and a jungle of hanging plants—and saying and doing sophisticatedly romantic things together. And when he got tired of that one, there was another about being world travelers, in which he pictured them walking hand in hand across picturesque bridges in ancient cities, stopping to look first at the view and then, passionately, at each other, and then hurrying back to make love until the first rays of morning sun crept through the wrought iron balcony beyond their window in the quaint seventeenth century hotel.

It was during those days of wine and roses that Charlotte obviously stopped being concerned about the state of James' emotions and William suddenly began to take an interest. Charlotte, it seemed, had told him about Diane, and it turned out that William knew something about the Jarretts. It figured. If there was one thing James had always been able to count on his father for, it was that he would know something about any subject that might happen to come up. In the case of the Jarretts, he'd learned about them from Dan Willowby, Ph.D., professor of environmental studies and author of several books on ecology and conservation, and of course, the present owner of the Willowby cabin. It semed that Henry Jarrett, Diane's father, had been one of the original backers of Major T. J. Mitchell's plan to develop the whole southern shore of New Moon Lake and turn it into The Camp. And, in the course of the early negotiations, Jarrett and Dan had had several meetings, or more strictly speaking, confrontations. After that, William said, Dan had gone on taking a special interest in the affairs of Hank Jarrett and had collected quite a bit of information on him.

"It would seem that as a contractor, Mr. Jarrett's record on ecological matters has left something to be desired," William said. "At least, according to Dan. But then Dan does tend to be a bit dogmatic where such things are concerned."

"Yes. I know," James said. Dr. Willowby was the type who would advocate relocating a fairly large city in order to protect the breeding grounds of a fairly common species of earwig.

"They met at a social function set up by Jarrett's people to recruit support among New Moon landowners. Can't you picture it? A doomed relationship, I'm afraid. It transpired that in addition to everything else, Jarrett is an avid hunter." William's smile invited James to enjoy the imagined scene—dedicated hunter meets dedicated conservationist.

James found himself beginning to feel a little bit defensive. He knew how Dr. Willowby felt about hunting, and he also knew how Dr. Fielding felt about it, and it wasn't all that much different. Except that William didn't quite go along with his friend's proposal that all hunters should be given licenses to hunt a more dangerous and expendable species—namely, each other. James' defensiveness increased when his father asked, "And your friend—Diane, I think your mother said her name was—

how does she feel about her father's interest in hunting."

James found himself saying, "I don't see why people like you and Dr. Willowby take the attitude that all hunters are just bloodthirsty killers. There are some good reasons for hunting, you know."

"Oh?"

James looked carefully for the sarcasm he felt must be lurking beneath his father's smile. "Yes," he said. "What about the species that have overbred because all their predators have been killed off, so that a lot of them would die of starvation if the hunters didn't keep down the overpopulation?"

William nodded. "Yes. It's quite true that some species would overproduce without some kind of human interference. But wouldn't it be better to have them harvested by teams of trained rangers? Professionals who would all be excellent marksmen and who would be less apt to be under the influence of extreme excitement and/or alcohol when they pulled the trigger. And who would take care to kill the weak and inferior specimens as nature does, rather than the most perfect, thus improving the species rather than weakening it as hunting does."

"But what about poor people who depend on hunting for part of their food supplies?" It didn't have anything to do with the Jarretts, of course, but it seemed like a good point; and anyone who argued with William Fielding needed all the good points he could get.

"Game killed by rangers could be given away; but even if it were sold, a great deal of it could be purchased for less money than most modern-day hunters spend on one hunting expedition."

James could feel his defensiveness turning into

anger, or something fairly close to it. It wasn't so much that he disagreed with what his father was saying. What he really resented was the way William always managed to back people into defending a position they didn't really believe in, and then went on smiling calmly without even noticing how the other person might be feeling.

"But as I've often said, James," William was going on, "the welfare of wildlife, as important as it is, is not my major concern in this matter. What I really worry about is the type of civilization that produces people who choose killing as a form of recreation."

James got up and went out on the veranda. He sat on the railing staring in the direction of the lake, but not seeing anything. He felt angry and uneasy, and the fact that he wasn't sure who or what was to blame only seemed to make him angrier. After a while he got up, went to his room and, a few minutes later, came out wearing his hiking boots and with his pocket bulging with bread and apples. Vaulting over the railing, he started down the path toward the lake. When he came to where the west gate path branched off, he stopped for a moment and stood looking down it, thinking about the various things he might be able to do with the next three or four hours. But in the end he went on, straight down the hill to the lake and then up through the gullies that led to the Peter's Creek crossing. He pushed himself, climbing at top speed, and in only a little over an hour he was sliding down the steep incline into the deer's valley.

The stag wasn't in the first meadow so, without stopping, James went on through the wooded area, across the second meadow and into the small, dense grove at the end of the box canyon. As he approached the spring, the anxiety that had accompanied him since he left the cabin sharpened and tightened. By the time he reached the spot from which the deer's favorite resting place was visible, he was actually holding his breath—and then stale air rushed out and in again, in a gasp of relief. He was there.

In spite of James' long absence, the deer seemed calmer, less tensely wary, than ever before. Getting to his feet without apparent haste, he tested the air for only a moment before he began to move slowly toward the spot where James was standing. At about twenty feet he stopped and waited until James had placed his offerings on the ground and begun to back away; and then he came on again, until he reached the food.

Sleek, powerful and yet superbly graceful, the stag managed to make even the eating of an apple an act of dignity and grace. His antlers were smooth and burnished now, free of the last tatters of velvet, and his body seemed thicker and more muscular. The apples went down quickly, but the bread, rye this time, seemed to require discriminating inspection and thoughtful, head-tossing tasting. When the last bit of food was gone, he retreated a few steps and then stopped and half turned, presenting a magnificent silhouette.

James wished he'd remembered his camera. He'd photographed the stag several times before, but not recently, not since he'd been coming so close. Raising his hands, he pressed an imaginary button, attempting to impress the scene on a mental camera so indelibly that it would never be lost.

"You are really something, old man," he whispered.

The broad ears twitched, the crowned head tossed and one slender foreleg pawed the earth. "Okay. Okay, your majesty. I get it. The audience is over," James said, retreating to the edge of the grove. Among the trees he stopped once more to look back, in time to see the deer, legs gathered, subsiding onto his soft bed of pine needles.

Back at the flat boulder, James climbed up, stretched out and contemplated the sky. He thought briefly of his argument with William and of the hectic excitement of the last few days with Diane, but gradually as he lay quietly with his eyes wide open, the pure blue immensity above him seemed to flow down to fill his eyes and mind and seep through his veins, filling his whole body with peaceful calm. The silence was so complete that after a while it began to seem like a sound in itself, a pure, clear pulsing sound like the distant ringing of a great golden bell. Thoughts and feelings about people and events blurred and blended with the blue purity and the golden silence. And all of it, the silence and the calm and a strange whispering promise, began to seem like a mysterious gift that in some strange way came from the hidden valley and the stag sleeping quietly in his secret grove.

After a long time he rolled over on his stomach and with his chin on his fists, began to take a long last look around the valley, as he always did before starting back to the outside world. Everything was as it had always been—the meadow, the crouching boulders, the circling trees and behind them the sheer gray cliffs. But then, as he leaned forward to look down into the miniature jungle of meadow grass at the base of his boulder, he suddenly stiffened with amazement. Directly below his head a circular area had been cleared of grass and outlined by a ring of shiny pebbles, and in the midst of the cleared area, on a small pyramid of stones, there stood a small bronze deer. Of course, he realized immediately who was responsible.

CHAPTER 12

I T WAS late afternoon and there was only one car in the driveway when he knocked at the side door of the Westmoreland's A-frame. It was opened by a stranger, a young woman wearing a kerchief over her hair, a flowered smock over her slacks and a dust mop over her arm. Surprise rendered James momentarily speechless. There certainly wasn't anything surprising about her appearance. In fact, it was her extreme ordinariness that created the shock, in the context of the Westmoreland's pop-art super-trendy decor.

With calm efficiency the young woman simultaneously looked James over, tucked the dust mop under her arm, adjusted her kerchief and chewed a cheekful of gum. "Yes?" she said at last without breaking the brisk rhythm of her jaws; and then, "The Westmorelands aren't home, except for the kids."

"Oh—well—actually I came to see the kids," James said. "That is, I came to see Griffin—Griffith, that is. I'm James Fielding."

"Oh, okay. I'll see if I can find her. She's around here someplace." She started to close the door but after scrutinizing James again carefully, apparently decided he looked harmless. "Would you like to come in?"

Seated on one of the transparent chairs, James had been waiting for several minutes when Griffin came into the room. She was wearing jeans, a faded cotton shirt and was, as usual, barefooted. But now that Charlotte had mentioned it, he could see a slight resemblance to her mother. What had seemed only odd before, from a different perspective could be seen as an unfinished version of exotic elegance. As she saw James, her surprising smile lit up her face.

When the young woman, whom Griffin introduced as Cynthia-our-new-live-in, left the room, James got right to the point and Griffin admitted everything. Yes, she had been going to the valley since he'd taken her there. James was indignant. "I didn't say you could go there by yourself," he said.

"Oh, I don't go by myself," she said. "Woody and Laurel go with me."

"Woody and Laurel!" He was not only indignant but aghast as well. "Look. That is very, very dangerous."

"Dangerous?" She didn't seem to know what he was talking about. "What's dangerous about it?"

"Well, the cliff trail in the first place. That whole stretch just before you get to the top. If you fell from there, you'd be lucky to live through it."

"But we're very careful, all of us. I make sure the kids are very careful."

"And it's not just the cliff. It's the deer, too. He *is* a wild animal and a very powerful one, too. He's never shown any sign of wanting to hurt me, but you never really know what a wild animal is going to do. Particularly around little kids. If they annoyed him or made him feel cornered—"

She was shaking her head, smiling knowingly. "He won't hurt them," she said.

"How can you be sure?"

"I'm sure."

He looked at her carefully. She was wrong, of course. There was no way anyone could be sure about a think like that. She obviously didn't know what she was talking about, but she looked so calmly confident you could almost believe she did. He decided to change his approach.

"And it's dangerous for him, too, for the deer. You can't count on kids that young keeping their mouths shut. I guess Woody's fairly safe. At least, he's usually around where you can keep your eye on him, but Laurel . . ." He shook his head. "Around all those other Jarretts—and she must know how much they'd love to get their hands on him . . ."

Griffin was almost laughing. "Laurel wouldn't tell. Nothing in the whole world could make Laurel tell."

"I don't see how you can be so sure."

She looked thoughtful. "I don't know," she said uncertainly. "I guess it's just that I know her so well. I know what she's thinking and how she feels about everything."

He shrugged impatiently. He supposed she thought she knew what the deer was thinking and how it felt about things, too. The thought angered him. He had been the one who had found the deer and who had slowly and patiently trained it to accept his presence.

"How many times have you been there?" he asked.

"To the stag's valley?"

"Yes. How many times have you taken the kids there?"

"I'm not sure. Seven or eight times, or maybe nine. Every day but one, I think, since you took me there."

He shook his head letting his expression say that he wasn't going to swallow that one. He was definitely getting the impression that Griffin was indulging in one of her creative narratives. "That would mean you've been gone three or four hours out of every day—more than that probably with little kids along, and nobody's noticed? Don't your parents ever check up on you? And how about Laurel's parents?"

"Laurel's parents have gone to Europe. And Susie, that's her sitter, has been very busy with a new boyfriend lately. She lets Laurel leave every day at nine o'clock because her boyfriend's the new life guard, and that's when she goes to meet him at the pool. So we meet at the Nymph's Grove every day at nine thirty, and then we go to see the Stag. And it doesn't matter about our parents. They don't care how much time we spend in the woods. They know I'll take good care of Woody."

"Griffin." Cynthia had come back into the room carrying a wastepaper basket. "You'd better go see about Woody. He's sitting up in that tree out back, crying. He won't talk to me, but I think he's afraid to climb down."

Griffin jumped up and ran from the room, and Cynthia flopped down into a chair and began tucking strands of hair back under the red kerchief, while she looked at James with frank curiosity.

"Do you live here at The Camp?" she asked.

He explained about the Willowby arrangement and

about how he didn't really know the Westmorelands except that he'd met the kids and he just dropped by to ask Griffin a question.

"Oh, yes," she said. "I know about the Willowby place. We used to hike up there a long time ago, before they built this place and cut off the path. I live in New Moon. That is, I did until I moved into this"—she gestured with both arms—"madhouse."

"Madhouse?"

She shrugged. "Well, in a manner of speaking. Crazy parties and all kinds of weird people. Oh, the kids are all right, Griffin and Woody. A little weird, but all right. But some of the rest of them—"

"Crazy parties?" James prompted.

She raised her eyebrows and rolled her eyes. "Crazee!" she said. "Like, a couple of days ago the house was full of people, and one of them was some sort of guru who had everyone taking some kind of dope and lying around contemplating their own deaths. And last week it was a woman who supposedly was going to teach everyone to levitate. By the time that party was over, hardly anyone was on their feet, all right, but it wasn't because they were floating, at least not physically."

James couldn't help grinning. "It does sound pretty far out."

"Far out doesn't even touch it. I told my fiancee about some of the things that go on here, and he wants me to quit right away. But we need the money, and besides, I don't really have to have anything to do with any of the people here except the kids. I'm just supposed to be around to see that they get fed and that sort of thing, and to be here with them at night. I don't even have to cook when their parents are here. They always bring their own help with them. It's really an easy job."

"Yes, I guess it would be. And I suppose the kids aren't much trouble. That is, they're off on their own pretty much during the day, aren't they?"

Cynthia looked at him sharply. "Yeah," she said. "They like to play in the woods. Mrs. Westmoreland said it was all right to let them." The friendly expression had been replaced by a defensive suspicion, as if she were suddenly seeing James as a spy for the Westmorelands —someone who'd been sent to make sure she was doing a good job. "Mrs. Westmoreland said the kids have always practically lived in woods whenever they were here at The Camp. She said she didn't know how she happened to produce a couple of aborigines." Cynthia leaned back languidly and flourished an imaginary cigarette in a dramatic gesture. "I can't explain it, darling. They certainly didn't get it from me. A sidewalk cafe is about as outdoorsy as I care to get." She checked the effect of her pantomime on James and then added firmly. "She didn't say *anything* about making them stop."

"Hey look," James said. "It's okay with me. It's probably the best place for them. I mean, I think nature is great for kids."

"Hi, Prince. Hi." Woody ran into the room, tear-streaked, grungy and more gap-toothed than ever.

"Hi, Woody. Looks like you've been keeping the tooth fairy busy."

"Yeah," Woody stuck his tongue into the latest vacancy. "You know where I was, Prince? I was clear up to the Eagle's Lair."

"The Eagle's Lair?"

"Yeah. We have this great climbing tree out back and all the different places in it have special names. Like the Dragon's Landing and the Crow's Nest and the Eagle's Lair. And you have to be a very good climber to get to the Eagle's Lair, and I never could, only today I did it." Woody's triumphantly lifted chin tucked suddenly. "But then I didn't feel like coming down all by myself and Grif went off and left me." He stopped to glare at Griffin, who had followed him into the room.

"You should have let Cynthia help you down," Griffin said.

Woody's glare got more ferocious. "She couldn't help me. She doesn't know anything about tree climbing."

Cynthia snorted. "That's what I like," she said. "Appreciation. Makes it all worth while." She got up and headed for the kitchen. "Dinner will be in about half an hour," she called over her shoulder.

James looked at his watch. "I've got to be getting home. Griffin, could I talk to you a minute? I mean, alone?" There were a couple of points he felt still needed emphasizing.

Having persuaded Woody with some difficulty to stay where he was, Griffin walked with James to the end of the drive. On the way he warned her again about the importance of impressing on the kids the absolute necessity of keeping quiet about the deer. Particularly Laurel. "And when her parents come back from Europe you'd better stop taking her there, at least so often. They'd be sure to get suspicious." For a moment he considered mentioning the conversation he'd overheard between Jill and Angela Jarrett.

He'd just decided not to mention it when Griffin said, "I know. Her parents don't like her being with Woody and me so much. But they won't be home until it's almost time for school to start anyway. And then none of us will be here anymore."

Somehow he kept forgetting the summer was nearly over. "When will your parents be back?" he asked.

As always, her face seemed to close down as if some kind of internal fires had gone out, or springs dried up. "I'm not sure. Not very long. They've gone home, to our house in San Francisco."

"Home? They've gone home and left you and Woody here?" He tried to make his tone of voice invite her to tell him more.

Instead she only turned her head so he couldn't see her face. Her voice sounded tight, tense or perhaps angry. "They'll be back soon. They just went down for a party. And to see a doctor. My mother had to see a doctor. And we didn't want to go."

"Is your mother sick?"

"Yes," she said quickly, and then, "Well, not sick exactly. It's the pain because of the accident. The accident when my father was killed. She almost got killed, too, and ever since she has to take medicine for the pain."

The tension was still there; but without being able to see her face, it was hard to tell just what it was about. "Well, look," James said. "I've got to go now. Don't forget what I said—about the deer."

"I won't. We won't." She was facing him again, standing at attention, her level eyes intense as laser beams. "We will not tell anyone about the stag. Not anyone. Not ever."

It sounded like a pledge of allegiance. He turned away, and when he had his grin under control, he looked back and waved. She was still standing stiffly at attention, but her face was back to normal—as full of activity as a three ring circus.

The next morning James had an early date for a game of tennis with Diane. For once she was there right on time, but as soon as the game was over she said she had to go home. There was no time, she said, for a hike in the woods, however short. He tried to argue, but it didn't do any good and a few minutes after ten he found himself on his way back to Willowby cabin. He spent the first half of the walk home worrying about Diane—she'd seemed a little bit distant again—but then he found himself thinking about the deer. About the deer and Griffin and the kids and whatever it was they'd been doing every day in the valley. He ate an early lunch, left a note for his parents, who had gone for a walk on the lake-shore, and by twelve o'clock was well on his way.

It wasn't until he'd slid down the slope into the first meadow without seeing anyone, or being seen, that he decided to play the spy. If the kids weren't there already, they would probably be arriving soon, and either way he could observe them for a while without being seen if he were careful. Sinking into a crouch—James Fielding, super-spy—he zigzagged across the meadow, dodging from boulder to boulder, and crept into the shelter of the surrounding trees. He circled the second meadow, staying among the heavy underbrush near the base of the cliff, and had almost reached the small, dense grove that surrounded the spring, when he suddenly stopped and then crept forward more carefully than ever. He had definitely heard the sound of human voices.

He saw the little kids first. Woody and Laurel were sitting cross-legged, straight-backed, near the base of a large tree, like a couple of small buddhas. They were looking away from him, staring intently toward something beyond his field of vision. Dropping back, he circled among tree trunks to a spot more directly behind them. They were facing a small treeless area, a clearing that James recognized as being very near the deer's resting place. Like spectators waiting for a performance to begin, they were sitting quietly, their hands in their laps.

He eased closer, so close that when Woody leaned toward Laurel, he clearly heard his loud stage whisper. "What's she doing? Why is it taking such a long time?"

"Shh," Laurel said. "She's getting ready."

They went on sitting quietly except that now Laurel had turned her attention to something she was holding in her lap. Woody scooted closer, watching what she was doing. James was maneuvering, trying to get to where he could see too, when looking up he caught his breath in surprise.

Griffin was standing in the center of the clearing. It was Griffin all right, although for just a fraction of a second he hadn't been sure. She was wearing a short white tunic, and her hair hung loose and thick around her shoulders and down to well below her waist. There was a wreath of green leaves on her head and bracelets of flowers around her wrists and ankles. She was holding what seemed to be a silver punch bowl at arms length.

"Ohh. Look," Laurel whispered.

Very slowly Griffin raised the bowl higher and as she lifted her head, the heavy shawl of hair shifted and slid, gleaming palely in the rays of green-tinged sunlight. For a brief moment James found himself capable of a kind of Griffinesque double-vision—capable of seeing a kooky kid playing a fantastical game and, at the same time, watching in a kind of awe as some magical creature of the forest, something pure and free and beautiful, moved through a ritual of strange significance.

She knelt, then, and placing the bowl on the ground, she dipped her hands in it and lifted them to her face. As she bent over the bowl, the pale curtains of her hair swung down around it, and between the curtains, water fell in glistening drops and shone on her face as she rose to her feet. As she moved towards the children, James drew back among the tree trunks.

"Give me the talismans," he heard her say.

She took something from each of them, small, oblong objects attached to long red ribbons, and turned to go.

"No wait," she said as the children started to get to their feet. "Not yet. I'll come back for you when it's time." She crossed the clearing and disappeared in the direction of the spring.

The wait seemed long, but it might have been no more than fifteen or twenty minutes. Woody fidgeted, stretched out at full length on the pine carpeted ground, and then sat up and put a pine cone down the back of Laurel's blouse. Obviously making a valiant effort to maintain a faithful vigil, Laurel had managed to ignore Woody until the pine cone incident when, after fishing it out, she threw it at him, thumped him on the head with both fists and then went quickly back to her modified lotus position. Woody waved a fist in her general direction in an unconvincing threat of reprisal, and then settled for a less physical attack. "You're not doing it right," he said. "Your feet are on wrong."

"I know it," she said. "They just won't bend that way. Yours aren't right either."

"They almost are. See. Mine are better than yours." Woody was still trying to pull a sneaker-clad foot up onto his thigh when Griffin suddenly reappeared. Her face was glowing with a wild excitement.

Woody jumped to his feet. "Did you do it? Did he let you do it?"

She nodded hard, mouth tight, eyes blazing. "Quick," she said. "Get the offering."

Woody disappeared from James' range of vision and returned a moment later with a large paper bag. Emptying the water from the silver bowl Griffin poured in the contents of the bag, which seemed to be some kind of grain. When she shook the bowl from side to side, the grain made a soft sifting noise.

"Now," she said. "Hurry." They sat again, all three of them now, at the base of the tree—cross-legged, arms extended, palms upward, eyes tightly closed. "Send for him. Send the invocation," Griffin said.

Woody's lips began to move in exaggerated slow motion as he mouthed the words of what was obviously some kind of ritual chant. Watching him, James was beginning to grin when a sudden sound drew his attention and he looked up to see something so amazing that he forgot not only about Woody, but also what he was doing, himself. Without knowing how he got there, he found himself standing next to Griffin, staring in amazement as the deer entered the clearing. Pausing only for a moment, he came on to the silver bowl and then lowered his crowned head—a crown that was now decorated with fluttering red ribbons.

CHAPTER 13

THERE followed several days during which James spent a great deal of time thinking. Actually, there wasn't much else to do. He'd finally finished the da Vinci essay and sent it off to Mr. Johnson, and he suddenly wasn't spending nearly as much time with Diane.

He wasn't entirely sure just why. When he did see her, things were just as great, or almost as great, as ever. The only difference was that they spent a lot more time in public places—at the tennis courts, or swimming pool, or anyplace where people tended to congregate—and a lot less time on hikes in secluded places. But other times when he called up she said she couldn't see him right then. Usually there was some good reason, or at least some reason that sounded reasonable. Like for instance, she had to go in to Tahoe with her mother to shop for a new bathing suit, which, in spite of the fact that she already owned at least a dozen, sounded like something you'd expect a girl to do. And she always sounded as if she were sorry about not being able to see him.

A couple of times when they'd finally gotten to-gether after several unsuccessful attempts on his part, he'd come right out and asked her if there was anything wrong, and if she still felt the same way about him. Her answers had always been extremely reassuring.

"Jamesy," she'd say, "how can you ask such a silly question? Can't you tell how I feel about you? Come here and let me show you." And she would drag him off (not that he ever resisted much) around a corner or behind the nearest tree, and they would mess around until he'd forgotten his worries completely. At least his worries about Diane. After such sessions behind the corner of the Commissary or the big sycamore on the Parade Grounds, his problems tended to be more physical than anything else. Physical and embarrassing. Not that it ever seemed to embarrass her. In fact she seemed to think it was all pretty amusing, particularly the time he'd had to sit down quickly at a picnic table because some peo-ple were coming along the path right toward where they were. That time he hadn't thought it was all that funny. However the next time Diane wanted to mess around in a semi-public place, he hadn't exactly refused. And later, during one of the long periods when he had nothing to do but think, he'd gotten over feeling irritated at her for laughing at him.

He'd also had time to do quite a bit of thinking about Griffin and the deer and what had been going on in the hidden valley. He still hadn't quite gotten over the shock of finding out that Griffin was able to go right up to him, touch him, and even tie things on his antlers. After weeks of careful and patient and maddeningly slow progress, he had earned the right to come to within approximately twenty feet, but no closer, and now in a period of a few days she'd actually been able to put her hands on his wild deer. He still found it hard to believe, although she'd told him all about how she'd done it that day on their way home from the valley.

After they had safely gotten past the cliff trail, which Woody and Laurel had crossed with surprising skill and fearlessness, Griffin had made them run on ahead so she and James could talk.

"How did you get him to let you do it?" he'd asked her. "I'm really amazed."

"I don't know exactly." Griffin looked worried as if she were afraid he was really upset, which of course, he wasn't, or at least not very much. "I guess it was just that you'd already tamed him so much that he wasn't really all that much afraid any more. So it was easier for me."

He shrugged. "Well maybe. But I still can't understand it. In less than two weeks he lets you walk right up and touch him. You and two noisy little kids."

"Oh no," Griffin said. "I can't do it when the kids are around. He always keeps his distance when they're with me. I have to be all alone, and everything has to be just right."

James grinned. "So that's it. That's what I was lacking. No olive wreath and Grecian toga."

She looked embarrassed. "It wasn't really. Just bay leaves and Wes' old tee shirt. See." She indicated the oversized tee shirt that was now tucked into her jeans. "But the rest of it was real. The ceremony was the important part, and that was real."

"The ceremony?"

She nodded. "The Ceremony of the Talismans Against Evil. It was Laurel's idea, at least at first. After I told them what you said about how all the hunters would want to shoot the stag if they knew about him, she started to worry like crazy."

"Laurel does everything like crazy," James said.

Griffin smiled. "I know. But she was really nervous about the stag, so we decided to have a ceremony to give him magical protection from hunters, or anyone who might want to hurt him. We made the amulets and did a lot of ceremonies to make them powerful, but I didn't know if he'd really let me tie them to his antlers. I'd touched him before, though just barely. But the ceremony worked. Do you want to hear about the ceremony?"

James said he did, so she'd gone into the whole thing in great detail. There had been a fast, necessitating elaborate maneuvers to keep Cynthia from realizing her charges weren't eating. And then, after having reached the valley, a ritual had been performed that would bring down a curse on anyone who planned to harm the stag. Then the kids had been stationed where he'd found them, while Griffin had gone off alone to prepare for her part in the final ceremony. The part James had witnessed had been the Purification of the High Priestess.

"I thought it was something like that," he said. "That was very impressive. Why don't you leave your hair loose like that all the time?"

"My hair?" They were walking along a narrow stretch of trail at the time, with Griffin in the lead, and he saw her hand go back to touch her hair, a single braid again hanging down the middle of her back. She stopped suddenly and turned back, looking puzzled. "Why did you say that? About my hair?"

"Why? Because I like the way it looked. You have beautiful hair."

To his surprise her cheeks actually got red and her dark brows drew together in a frown that looked almost painful. Whirling around, she began to run on the rocky, treacherous trail. He watched in amazement as she ran like a frightened deer on the narrow path, the long braid whipping behind her. She slowed down finally, but for a long time she maintained the distance between them.

Kooky kid, he thought. He wanted to ask her what was wrong, but not enough to run after her on terrain like that. There were, in fact, several more things concerning Griffin that he wanted to know more about. Things like why she reacted as she did to any mention of her home life, particularly if her mother was concerned. He had some theories about it. There was obviously a lot of anger involved. One of those love-hate things, no doubt: fascinated by her gorgeous mother, and at the same time hating her for spending all her time with her jet-set friends and neglecting her family. Perhaps hating her for a lot of other reasons, too. Given some of the off-beat things he'd heard about the Westmorelands, he could imagine a lot of reasons why Griffin might resent her mother and stepfather. But most of his ideas were based on imagination, without much definite proof. It would be interesting to discuss it with Griffin and find out how many of his guesses were correct. But it wasn't likely that he'd be able to, not while she went on freezing up at any mention of her mother. He decided however that if the opportunity arose, he would try again.

And not just to satisfy his own curiosity. It would probably be a good thing for her. Get all that pent-up anger and hatred out in the open.

It was on a Saturday morning, only one week before the Fieldings were due to leave New Moon Lake, that James arrived at the snack bar phone booth a little earlier than usual. It was the last Saturday in August, and in the town of New Moon there was to be a Farewell Festival. A farewell to the summer and all the summer tourists. There was to be a parade, all kinds of craft and game booths and even a fun house, which local craftsmen had constructed in an abandoned hardware store. Just three days earlier, when he had last seen Diane, she had said the fair sounded like fun in a corny hick-town way, and would James like to hike over with her on Saturday morning? Except for the fact that there were other more private places he'd prefer to visit with her, there was, of course, nothing he'd like better. And he said so, as far as he could remember, in perfectly straightforward, un-ambiguous, one syllable words. But when Diane answered the phone that morning, she did it again—pulled the same old routine about not knowing they'd made it definite.

"Oh, we didn't say for sure did we? I thought you said you thought it would be too corny."

"You were the one who said it would be corny," he said, trying to keep the anger out of his voice until he knew for certain how things were going to turn out, because he knew from experience that one sarcastic comment and he would have blown it for sure.

"Oh, really? Are you certain? Because the way I remember it, you said you thought the whole thing would be pretty dumb. But anyway, Jamesy, the thing is, my dad just arrived for the weekend and he wants the whole family to go to the big event together. There's going to be some big deal ceremony that my dad has to go to. The city fathers are going to give Dad and old T.J. the keys to the city or some dumb thing like that, because of all the extra business since they built The Camp. You know, one of those, 'Ladies and Gentlemen. It gives me great honor to present . . .' sort of things. It'll be really dumb, but you know how parents are about things like that."

James knew, he guessed, but he wasn't happy about it.

"It's going to be an absolutely petrifying bore," Diane went on, "and besides, it's going to be too hot to hike all that way today, anyway. So why don't you just call me tomorrow morning and we'll do something then. Okay? Could you maybe call me again tomorrow?"

Glumly he agreed that *maybe* he could call her tomorrow. *Maybe*, he said, but he knew of course that there wasn't any *maybe* about it. Not the ghost of a paper-thin shred of a particle of a maybe. If there was any chance at all of seeing her, he'd call, and the trouble was—she knew it.

He hung up the phone, thought about going into the snack bar for a chat with Fiona and decided against it. He was in no mood to talk to anyone. With no definite destination in mind, he drifted across the Parade Grounds and out towards the big trees in the bivouac area. It was going to be hot, all right. Hot and bright and dry, and he couldn't think of a single thing he wanted to do. Diane was gone, for the day at least; and when he thought about the valley and the deer, it occurred to him that some things were gone there, too. The secret was gone and the exclusiveness and solitude. If he'd only kept his stupid mouth shut, he could go there now and stretch out on the boulder and let the clean blue silence seep into him and wash away the fiery whirlpools that seemed to be churning around in various parts of his anatomy. But he hadn't kept his mouth shut, and as a result he probably couldn't stretch out anywhere in the whole valley without being stepped on by little kids, or a skinny little kook in a tee shirt toga, leading his stag around on a red ribbon.

Realizing that he was hot, seething, boiling hot, in fact, he drifted towards the nearest tree, the big sycamore with the circular picnic table around its trunk. He climbed up onto the table and sat down, with his back against the trunk and his legs stretched out in front of him. It was somewhat cooler under the huge tent of overhanging limbs, but it didn't seem as if his internal temperature was dropping much.

Making an effort to get his mind off the things that were driving him up the wall, he started looking around for something to put it on instead. He watched a chubby kid in plaid shorts tearing around the soccer field on a red Motocross bicycle with knobby tires and rabbit-ear handlebars, and two typically well-groomed Camp matrons on their way to the tennis courts. Then a couple of cars approached on the road to the main gate, which crossed the bivouac area only a few yards from where he was sitting. The first car was a very slow moving station wagon with two women in the front seat and a swarm of little kids in the back—probably on their way to the New Moon Fair; and the next car, which was obviously being held to a crawl by the station wagon, was Lance Richardson's Porsche with the top down. And sitting so close to Lance that she was practically in his lap was Diane.

The strange thing was that it didn't make him angry, at least not right away. He wasn't angry, and he wasn't hot anymore, either. In fact what he felt right at first was cold and numb and a little like something had just hit him hard in the pit of the stomach. He got down off the picnic table very slowly and carefully, as if he were afraid a jolt of any kind might fracture something that had suddenly gone thin and brittle somewhere in his interior, and started walking slowly back toward the center.

He was passing the snack bar when he realized his throat felt strange, tight and dry, so he ordered a Dr. Pepper at the sidewalk window and sat down at one of the outdoor tables. He stayed there thinking for a long time. What he was thinking about was how it might have happened. How Diane might not really have been lying to him, even though at first glance it seemed as if she had been. There were several possibilities. Perhaps, for instance, Lance had just happened to drop by the Jarretts' just as they were all getting ready to go to the fair, and Diane had suddenly decided to ride over with him, since she had to go anyway. That seemed the best explanation, and the one he kept coming back to over and over again.

He'd been sitting there long enough for the shade from the metal umbrella to have moved without his noticing, when somebody said, "Hey, you trying to get sunstroke or something?"

Mike Jarret, in swimming trunks and a beach towel, was standing beside him drinking a Coke. Putting his Coke on the table, he pulled up a chair and sat down. James moved out of the sun.

Conversation wasn't as difficult as he would have expected and actually was a kind of relief. They talked about the hot weather, the fact that Mike was on his way to the swimming pool, and then James brought up the subject of the fair in New Moon.

"I hear your father's going to be given the keys to the city or something like that," he heard himself saying cooly. "Aren't you going to be there to watch?"

Mike grimaced. "I'll be there all right, if I know what's good for me. By special invitation of my old man. An offer I couldn't refuse."

"Well aren't you going to be late?"

"Late? It doesn't start until three-thirty this afternoon."

"Oh? I got the impression it was going to be earlier. Diane said she had to be there for the presentation, and I just happened to notice her leaving a little while ago."

Mike looked at him for quite a long time before he said anything. "You did, huh? You saw her leaving—with Lance?"

James nodded. He felt certain his face didn't show anything, but he wasn't sure what his voice would be like.

"Look, kid," Mike said, which fortunately irked James enough to burn out whatever it was that was threatening his vocal chords. More than irked, actually. He happened to know that Mike was barely seventeen. "Look, kid. Don't worry about that jerk and his Porsche. It won't last. For one thing, Richardson goes through dames like a chain smoker through a pack of Kools. And he's not really interested in Di. She's been after him and his cars for years, and he's always treated her like a little kid. Which really drives her crazy." He grinned in a way that he probably meant to be sympathetic but which made James want to hit him in the mouth. Which was a feeling he couldn't remember ever having had before, at least not since he was about ten years old. "It won't last," Mike said again. "I know what I'm talking about."

Afterwards, thinking back about the whole scene, James could remember smiling cooly and reminding himself not to hit his head on the metal umbrella when he stood up, which he usually did and which, under the circumstances, would have been just about the last straw. But after that he couldn't remember a thing about leaving The Camp and getting back to the Willowby cabin.

The period that followed was unlike any he had ever known. He went through all the routines—getting up, eating, going out into the woods at least far enough to get away from Charlotte's worried gaze, coming back to sit holding an unread book—with a curiously detached feeling, as if some important part of him was missing.

For the first time in his life he found himself feeling nostalgic. He found himself, lying in bed, twenty-three days before his sixteenth birthday, looking back wistfully on the days of his youth. On a time when a wakeful period meant leading an army of elephants over the alps, or attacking the sheriff in Sherwood Forest, instead of providing a forum for an idiotic debate over whether Diane was a clever, sneaky cheat, or a beautiful, reckless, exciting person.

And then one morning, when his defenses had been weakened by a particularly sleepless night, Charlotte struck. She waited until William had gone down to the lake for his morning dip, and then she started making gentle sympathetic hints about what he was going through, and it worked. He broke down and told her all about it—all of it, right down to the Porsche and the things Mike had said at the snack bar, and how he didn't need to be told he was being an imbecile because he knew it, and that knowing it didn't help a bit.

She waited until he was all through before she said anything and then, instead of saying anything useful, all she did was start telling him a long story that had nothing to do with him at all. The story was about how, when she was in college, she'd fallen in love with the quarterback of the football team—a handsome, macho, charismatic guy with whom she had absolutely nothing in common, but whom she would probably have married if he hadn't had the good sense to jilt her for another girl.

"We couldn't have been more wrong for each other," she said, "and in a way I knew it, and yet I was absolutely mindlessly in love with him."

She stared out the window for a minute without saying anything, and then she sighed and went on. "Being in love!" she said. "It's something that happens to almost everyone at one time or other, and the strange thing is, it often seems to have very little to do with any personal qualities the love object might have that would make them a good lover or companion or even friend. But

James—there is one thing that I can tell you that is true and important."

He dropped his eyes because he didn't want her to see that he didn't believe her. She couldn't possibly know what was true for him because she couldn't possibly understand how he felt about Diane and how he was feeling now.

"You won't believe me," Charlotte said, "because when you're in love, particularly if it's the first time and even more so if you're quite young, you're absolutely positive that nobody ever felt the way you do. But I'll tell you anyway. The truth is—you'll get over it. You don't believe me, but you will. Everyone always does. It either turns into real love, which is something quite different, or it goes away. But in the meantime there are a couple of things you could do about it—and it doesn't seem to me that you're doing either one."

"Like what?" he muttered without looking up.

"You could do something to get her back, or you could put your mind on other things and start getting over her."

So in a way, what happened was Charlotte's fault—at least to the extent that it happened because he decided to take her advice. He decided, at first, to get over Diane—to put her out of his mind once and for all. He really tried, but after he'd been trying all the rest of that day and halfway through the next night, he gave up. He couldn't forget her, and he wasn't even sure he wanted to, so there was nothing left except the other possibility, which was trying to do something—anything at all—that might help to get her back.

The first step had to be to simply get her to see him.

To see him and really talk to him for more than just a few minutes. He had to do something to really get her attention . . .

He suddenly stopped tossing and turning, and for a long time lay very still. Then he turned on the light and went straight to his desk and opened the shoebox that held his da Vinci file. He found what he was looking for right where he had filed it several weeks before—under S for stag. It was a photograph that he had taken early in July.

CHAPTER 14

AFTER he'd decided to show Diane the picture of the deer, he felt better than he had in a long time. His plan was to show her the picture and simply tell her that he'd taken it somewhere in the general area of New Moon Lake. And of course, he wouldn't even do that until she'd promised not to tell anyone else.

He knew how fascinated she'd be. There wasn't the slightest doubt about that. There was sure to be a long debate on whether he was going to tell her exactly where he took the picture—and why he really couldn't. That part, as he saw it, would be especially important. Perhaps he would even be able to make her understand the deer's unique importance. His importance not just as an extraordinarily beautiful specimen, but also as a symbol of the past when, under the rule of natural selection, other magnificent specimens such as he lived into their prime and passed on their superior size and strength and intelligence to many descendants.

And perhaps, if things were going well enough and she seemed to be understanding, he could try to make her see what the deer had meant to him personally—a creature triumphantly wild and free that had accepted and trusted him and by doing so had made him a part of something mysterious and indescribable, but somehow totally important. And if he could make her understand that, it would prove that Charlotte was wrong, and that her story really didn't relate to his situation at all.

The phone conversation was very difficult, as he had feared it would be. Although he was careful to keep his voice very calm and unemotional, Diane immediately went on the offensive.

"Well, I thought you must have gone back to Berkeley or something, without even saying good-by."

"No," he said evenly. "We're not going until Friday. I've just been very busy. And I heard you were, too."

There was a pause. "Oh yeah?" she said at last. "Like, what did you hear, exactly?"

"What I heard isn't important, at least not now. That's not what I called about. What I called about is just that I'd like to come over to say good-by and—"

"Well," she interrupted, "in just a few minutes I've got to—"

"Wait a minute," he said. "Just let me finish. There's another reason why I want to see you. There's something I have to show you."

"Show me?"

"Yes. Something you've never seen anything like in your whole life, and probably never will again. Something you have a particular interest in—"

"Well, what is it? Why can't you just tell me what it is?"

"No. I can't do that. For one thing, before I show you, you have to promise not to tell anyone. Not anyone, not ever."

There was another pause, a longer one. At last Diane said, "Well, I don't have very much time, but maybe you could come up for just a few minutes. Would that be all right?"

"Yes, that would be all right. But it would be better if you could meet me somewhere."

"No. I can't do that. No one's home right now except me and Jacky. I'm baby-sitting him until Mom gets back from her hair appointment. So I can't go away."

"Okay," James said. "I'll be there in just a few minutes."

As he went up the driveway, she was leaning over the deck railing. She was wearing a tight black tee shirt and shorts made out of artificial tiger skin with yellow and black stripes. Her hair was different, more sophisticated looking, with two smooth wings sweeping back to an upturned fringe on each side of her head, and she'd done something new with makeup that made her eyelids look faintly blue. She looked older and sleeker and more sexy than ever. When he was halfway up the drive, she greeted him with a double fisted, "Ka-pow!" and when he got to the top of the stairs she took both his hands and kissed him. A brief kiss, but enough to make him think that so far everything was going better than he had dared to hope.

In the trophy room Jacky was curled up on one of the leather couches fast asleep; but when James started whispering, Diane told him not to bother.

"He just climbed up on the counter in the kitchen

and ate half a cookie jar full of rum balls," she said. "He won't hear you."

Not only Jacky's eyes, but his whole face looked squeezed shut and he was breathing very deeply. One pudgy pink fist was clamped around the golf ball so hard that the knuckles looked white.

"Is he all right?" James asked uneasily.

"Oh sure. He does it all the time. Stuffs himself and conks out. Like a boa constrictor."

She led the way to one of the other leather couches and sat down. "Okay. So what is it that you want to show me?" she said.

Of course, he made her promise first. Promise on her word of honor that she would never tell anyone. And then he took the picture out of his pocket and put it in her hands. She stared at it for a long time before she said anything. She turned it over, looked at the back, turned it back, stared at James for a moment and finally said, "Where did you get this?"

"I took it," he said.

"Where?"

"Not too far from here."

"Did you get close enough to count the prongs? It looks as if there must be ten or eleven."

"Twelve," James said.

She stared at him. "Are the points in more or less the same places on each side, or are they all uneven?"

"They're very symmetrical."

She shook her head muttering something under her breath. "When did you say you took this?"

"Early in July."

"I thought so. They look as if they were still in

velvet. They probably grew a little more after this was taken."

"A little," he said without thinking.

She looked up sharply. "You mean, you've seen it recently?"

"Well, I've seen him since then—since July."

"You've seen this buck more than once? In more or less the same place?"

He reached out suddenly and tried to take the picture out of her hands, but she held on to it. Still staring at it she said, "Do you realize what a—I mean, how unusual this buck is. They just don't ever live long enough to get to be like this anymore. Especially not in California. And this one would be amazing in Colorado or anywhere. My dad would go out of his mind."

He took the picture away and put it back in his pocket. "Listen, Diane," he said. "I have to tell you about this deer."

"Yes," she said, "tell me." She took both his hands and held them all the time he was talking.

He thought he did it pretty well—explained about the deer's importance as a beautiful part of nature, as a symbol of the wilderness as it once existed—and as a personal symbol, mysteriously significant. And as he talked she listened intently, even more intently than he had imagined she would, her eyes shining and her lips slightly parted.

When he finished she said, "That is *so* beautiful, Jamesy. The way you told that. And it's all so amazing. The way you really sort of tamed it. Tamed a wild buck. That's really an incredibly beautiful thing." Taking his face between her hands she kissed him hard, and, of course, he kissed her back. Then they went on kissing and each kiss was a separate swinging spiraling high, and if there was anything at all going on in his mind it was just a groggily exultant refrain that kept repeating itself over and over. "It worked. She does understand. It really worked and she really understands."

They might have gone on more or less indefinitely, but there was the sound of a car in the drive and then the slam of the back door, and Mrs. Jarrett's voice calling, "Di. Jacky."

When Diane called, "Here we are, Mom. Down here." Jacky started waking up, yawning and rubbing his eyes. James eyed him warily.

"I told you," Diane said, "he won't throw it at you anymore. You don't have to worry." But just as before James felt that Jacky's brown marble eyes were saying something not quite so reassuring.

Upstairs in the kitchen he chatted for a while with Jill Jarrett, who couldn't quite conceal her surprise at seeing him back in the running, and then Diane walked with him to the end of the drive. In their favorite grove they kissed again, but briefly because Diane said she really did have to get back to get ready for her diving lesson, and then they said, not good-by, but until tomorrow.

"Until tomorrow. Will I see you tomorrow?" Diane said.

"All right, tomorrow," he said. "What time should I come over?"

"Well, how about very early? Early enough so we

could go on a long hike. Could you, James? It would be so wonderful if you could take me to where you saw the deer."

There was a kind of shock, like a small jab of lightning. "I don't know," he said. "I don't think . . ."

"Please. If I promise and promise not to tell anyone?"

He didn't say yes, even though she begged him to with her hands folded, and then with her lips against his in a moist, "please, please, please." And finally, while tickling him all over and saying, "Say yes. Say yes. Or I'll never stop."

But he didn't tell her that he would take her to see the deer. All he actually said was that he'd think about it and tell her when he saw her tomorrow. And that evening he did think about it a lot more and decided that as much as he would like to tell her—and there was a part of him that definitely would—he couldn't and wouldn't do it.

It wasn't exactly that he didn't trust her. Or, if he didn't, he at least was able to explain and excuse her possible untrustworthiness in this particular area. He could understand how she might promise now, and really intend to keep her promise, not realizing how hard it would be and how much pressure she might be under at some time in the future. He could picture a situation when the Jarrets had returned to The Camp for the hunting season and when he, himself, wouldn't be there to remind her of her promise, and of a different set of values where the deer was concerned. There would be all the pressure of the competition to get the best trophy and the knowledge of what a bombshell she could drop by revealing the deer's existence. It would be just too much of a temptation. He finally went to sleep still trying to figure out the best way to break the news to her that they wouldn't be going on a hike, or at least not on that particular one, tomorrow morning.

He woke up early the next day, but he was still only half-dressed when he heard Charlotte calling him. A second later she knocked on his door and then stuck her head in.

"James. Oh, good. You're up." Her voice was matter of fact, but her face was making a surprised, quizzical comment of its own. "You seem to have company."

In the kitchen Diane was sitting at the table next to William, eating a piece of toast. After the few seconds it took him to get over his surprise, James made a stab at introductions, but Diane interrupted.

"Oh, never mind, James. We've already introduced ourselves. In fact, we've had enough time to get to be old friends, haven't we, Dr. Fielding."

Diane was wearing pants that fitted like Levi-colored skin and one of her famous tee shirts, and when she said, "Haven't we, Dr. Fielding," she leaned toward James' father and smiled one of her most dazzling smiles. And judging by his expression, William was dazzled, or at least a little astonished.

"Yes. Yes, indeed," he said, but then as Diane went on smiling at him he said, "Charlotte," and it sounded a little like a call for help.

Charlotte sat down by Diane and got her attention by passing her the toast plate. "Another piece of toast, Diane?" she asked.

"Oh no, thank you, Mrs. Fielding," Diane said. "I've

had plenty. And James and I really have to be going. We were planning to get a very early start, weren't we, James?"

"Well," James said. "I don't know—"

"That's all right. There's still time, and we forgive you for oversleeping. Just hurry and eat something so we can get started. Here. Sit down here and have some of this good toast."

He should have gotten things straightened out right then, at the beginning, instead of giving the impression he was going along with her plans: but it wasn't easy. Not with his mouth full of toast and with Diane chattering away about the wonderful farewell hike they'd planned to a great picnic spot way up near the top of the first ridge in the Six Prong range. She went on and on about it, describing their destination in such detail that it occurred to him that he hadn't really given her enough credit where imagination was concerned. In a very dramatic and vivacious way, she told about a waterfall and a beaver dam they hoped to see and how she had staggered out of bed at five-thirty that morning to make a picnic lunch for them. There wasn't really an opportunity for James to say anything at all; and by the time he'd finished eating, Charlotte and William were saying good-by and telling them to be careful, and they were out the door and on their way down the path.

He did try then, as soon as they were alone, to tell Diane about the decision he'd arrived at the night before, but she went on arguing and promising and coaxing in all kinds of persuasive ways, and somehow they kept on walking in the direction of the valley.

At one point he did stop dead in his tracks, when it suddenly occurred to him that they might run into Griffin and the kids. He hadn't told Diane about them, and he didn't intend to, because if she knew he'd already shared the secret, there would be absolutely no way he could refuse to tell her. But what almost stopped him was realizing how Griffin would feel if she knew he'd told Diane. They were almost to the river crossing when it hit him, and he sat down on a rock and began telling Diane that he'd just come to a firm decision. But then she sat down on his lap and started messing around and running her hands up and down his back and the back of his neck and kissing him, and in the midst of all that he remembered what Griffin had said about meeting Laurel at nine-thirty every morning. Glancing around Diane's head at his watch, he realized that if they hurried they could get into the valley, see the deer, and be back out again before Griffin and the kids reached the river crossing. Somehow, he just quit struggling, then, except for trying to get it over with in a hurry.

Things moved very quickly after that. Diane proved to be a surefooted and confident mountain climber, and she was very enthusiastic about the valley, particularly about the strange way the avalanche had cut it off so completely, except for the cliff trail. She kept talking about how amazing it was that James had managed to find it, and how impressed she was by his ability as a woodsman and explorer. And then they reached the flat boulder and almost immediately the deer came out into the meadow.

He stopped very briefly at the edge of the grove,

tested the air and then came on again. Leaving the shelter of the trees he moved confidently out into the morning sunshine, his fantastic head held proud and high. When he reached the center of the meadow, he stopped and waited—for the gift James had taught him to expect.

CHAPTER 15

WHEN the deer came out into the meadow Diane's reaction certainly left nothing to be desired. Where Griffin had only sat staring and chewing on her fingers, Diane raved. Clutching James' arm she babbled excitedly in disjointed sentences. The deer was wonderful, marvelous, unbelievable, one-in-a-million; and James was wonderful to have been able to tame him. Questions tumbled over each other. How had James managed to keep such a wonderful secret—what were those red ribbons on its horns—did it really let James tie them there—and why did he tie ribbons on its horns? Fortunately she never waited for an answer. Would it let her touch it—and, no, she didn't suppose it would—and she wouldn't really want to try—and how amazing it was that it would actually come when it heard people talking, and just stand there waiting like that only a few yards away.

"Waiting?" James said uneasily.

"To be fed," she said. "Here James, take him my cake, and my sandwich, too. Let's give him my sandwich. I don't want it."

So he fed the deer and then suggested that they ought to leave. He was afraid she'd want to stay and see the whole valley and watch the deer some more, but to his surprise she agreed without argument. On their way back across the cliff trail he checked his watch. They had been in the valley no more than twenty minutes.

Diane went on being particularly warm and friendly and agreeable most of the way home. When she wanted to stop to rest near the river crossing, he was able to convince her that he knew of a better place a little farther along. And when they got to the place he had in mind, safely away from the route Griffin and the kids would be taking, she continued to be affectionate, except that she never stopped talking. She went on and on about how wonderful the deer was and how grateful she was that she'd gotten to see him. Then she insisted that they eat the lunch she'd brought, even though it was only a little after ten. But when they'd finally run out of food and conversation, and James was trying to get some other things started, she suddenly got restless.

"I really ought to be starting home," she said. "My mother is packing today, and I promised I'd be back in time to help her. Come on, Jamesy. You can walk home with me. At least as far as the gate. Okay?"

So they said good-by at the west gate, and she kissed him five or six times and told him to call her in Sacramento and come to see her as soon as he could. And when he asked her to, she promised again that she would never tell anyone about the deer.

"At least, not until you're an old lady," he said. "When you're an old lady, you can tell your grandchildren about him. But no one before then. Okay?"

She put her arms around his waist and leaned back so the winglike fringes of blond hair fell back from the sides of her face. Raising her eyebrows in the way she always did when she was going to say something suggestive, she said, "Okay. When I'm an old lady, I'll tell *our* grandchildren all about it."

He laughed and tried to kiss her, but she ducked away and pushed the buzzer, and a moment later the guard was asking who went there, and Diane said she did, and then she was through the gate and disappearing among the trees.

When he got back to the cabin, William and Charlotte were just sitting down to lunch. "So *that* was Diane," Charlotte said, making a kind of stunned expression.

William was grinning too, in a very appreciative manner. "Very impressive,'" he said.

James tried not to look too pleased with himself. "Yeah," he said, shrugging. "That was Diane Jarrett, in the flesh."

His father chuckled. "Not a highly original turn of phrase," he said, "but in this case a singularly descriptive one."

James was starting to ask exactly what he meant by that when Charlotte interrupted. "Is she really only fifteen? She seems so—well, fully matured."

"I know. That's what I was trying to tell you."

"Yes, I know. But somehow I didn't get the full picture. Well, Max is certainly going to be impressed." Charlotte had always been amused by Max's world-famous-ladykiller routine.

"I know," James said grinning.

In fact that was one of the things he fantasized about that night—about Max's reaction when he met Diane. Lying there in bed on that next to the last night at New Moon Lake, he pictured Diane's first visit to Berkeley, and the conversation he would have with Max afterwards—a conversation in which Max would say he certainly wouldn't have wasted time feeling sorry for James for being carted off to the wilderness if he'd had any idea that the wilderness had terrain like that to explore.

The next morning he spent several hours helping his parents pack for the trip home. As usual when the Fieldings went anywhere, most of the luggage consisted of books and records and several dozen file boxes full of notes for William's latest book. By the time they'd finished, the poor old Volvo was sagging on its springs.

James pushed hard all morning, determined to get his part of the packing done early in order to have most of the day for his own personal good-bys. Diane had said her family had all sorts of last-minute things scheduled and she probably wouldn't be able to see him, but that he should at least call if he got to The Camp. He was planning to do that first. Then there was Fiona and, if possible, Griffin and company. And, of course, there was the stag. It would have to be a quick visit late in the day, but he really wanted to see him one more time to say good-by.

As seemed right and proper, Sergeant Smithers himself was manning the main gate to answer James' buzz and demand to hear his pass number: the whole ridiculous number, after an entire summer of opening the west gate on the average of twice a day for a James Fielding whose rather distinctive voice—youthful and yet masculine—had surely become familiar to him by now. James recited the number with gusto. It was an appropriate farewell gesture from The Camp—a momento to take back with him to the drab rationalism of the academic world.

He was still smiling—musing over Campish fads and fancies—when, in the middle of the Nymph's Grove, he came upon two of the people he was on his way to see —Griffin and Woody. He'd been walking quietly on soft soil, and for a moment they weren't aware of his presence. They were sitting on the ground facing away from him, down the path that led to Anzio and The Camp center. Woody was bent forward, his head resting on his knees, but Griffin sat erect with the thick pigtail looping her shoulder like a pet python.

Wondering what far-out fantasy they were involved in at the moment, James suddenly found himself ambushed by an unexpected combination of emotions. With some surprise he realized that Griffin and her two little disciples were among the things he was going to miss the most. He was really going to be sorry to say good-by; but he was glad that, at least, he was going to have a chance to say it. He was starting toward them when Griffin turned, saw him, and winced as if an invisible hand had struck her face; and although he didn't know, didn't even begin to guess what it was, he felt immediately that something very serious had gone wrong.

Her lips parted then, and she must have made some kind of sound because Woody raised his head. His freckled cheeks glistened wetly, and his long Griffith eyes were swollen and red. When he saw James, he jumped to his feet; and as James started towards him saying, "What is it? What's the matter?" Woody charged.

Head down and fists flailing, he crashed into James with the reckless ferocity of a banty rooster. Most of the blows went wild, but a few connected with surprising force before Griffith caught him from behind and pulled him away.

"What is it!" James gasped. "What got into him?"

With Griffin holding him tightly from behind, Woody was still swinging wildly in James' direction, gasping and choking and strangling on his own sobs. "You dirty traitor," he kept gasping. "You dirty traitor. You dirty son of a bitch traitor."

And suddenly, without knowing anything for certain and without any proof, James somehow knew what had happened. His own voice was out of control as he said, "What is it, Griffin? Tell me. What happened."

Her eyes shut him out, not with anger, but with a dazed hurt withdrawal that was a lot worse. Shaking her head she turned and, pushing Woody ahead of her, started down the path, but he ran after them, and grabbing her arms, forced her to stop. "You have to tell me," he said. "I have to know."

What followed was a crazy impasse that seemed to go on forever—with James holding Griffin, and Griffin holding Woody, and Woody sobbing and choking and trying to get at James with his fists and feet. At last Griffin looked at James and nodded stiffly. "All right. I'll tell you," she said. "Let me go."

He released her arm and stepped back, and she pulled Woody several yards down the trail before she stopped and bent over him, whispering. His sobs slowed to shuddering gasps; he turned to glower at James, and then nodded sullenly. "Okay," he said. "I won't. I won't anymore." Jerking away from Griffin, he threw himself face down on the ground and buried his face in his arms. Griffin knelt beside him and whispered for several minutes before she came back to where James was waiting.

She was there and yet not there. Standing robot-stiff, with her eyes still on Woody, she spoke in a dull monotone. "Laurel found out, last night when her uncle and aunt were having dinner at her house. She said her Uncle Hank talked about it all through dinner. About how Diane had found out about a fantastic buck. About how she'd sweet-talked a kid she knew into telling her where this smart old buck had been holing up. And how, unless Diane was exaggerating, he was going to make a trophy that would be nothing short of miraculous. He laughed about how smart Diane was. About how she held out on him, made him promise that she'd be the one who got to bag the buck, before she'd tell him where it was. And how they were going to be back at The Camp on the very first day of hunting season, and in the meantime he was going to see to it that Diane got in some good target practice, and how he was going to advise her to . . ." Griffin's voice faltered and then trembled as she went on, ". . . he was going to advise her to go for the lung shot because it was the surest in the long run and less apt to damage the trophy even though it did take a little longer to kill. And when Laurel started to cry, he told her not to feel bad because it was only a deer, and after the first shot it would be too stunned to feel much, even though it took him a while to die."

She stopped and breathed deeply several times until

her voice was under control again. "Laurel came to our house late last night. She'd been crying for a long time. I let her stay overnight, but this morning I made her go back before anyone found out. I told her we'd wait for her here in the grove today, but I don't know if she'll be able to come. Her folks are leaving for Sacramento this afternoon."

He heard every word Griffin said clearly and distinctly, but it was as if they somehow failed to register, or at least to have any immediate effect. At least not any that was appropriate and understandable. Instead there was only a cold, stiff paralysis that made him stand there without saying or doing anything while Griffin started away, turned back as if she were going to ask something, then changed her mind and went on. She went to where Woody was still lying, gathered him up and led him away down the trail. When they were out of sight, James went back to the Willowby cabin. By the time he was halfway there, the pain and anger had begun, and for a long time it got steadily and progressively worse. He sneaked back into his room, lay down on the bed and stayed there for the rest of the day. The stripped and empty room suited his mood. He didn't even consider going to the hidden valley. He tried very hard not to think about the deer at all.

CHAPTER 16

FORTUNATELY school started two days after the Fieldings returned to Berkeley, and James was terribly busy. Busier than he had ever been in his life. Besides carrying an extra-heavy academic load in order to complete two years of high school in one, he also signed himself up for every extra curricular activity he could cram into his schedule. He wasn't entirely sure why.

On the most obvious level it might just have been an attempt to keep himself so busy he would have less time to think, but there were times when he thought he detected motives that were even more ulterior. For instance, he couldn't imagine why he would have signed himself up for two afternoons a week of touch football, unless it was some obscure desire to suffer for his sins.

He was limping home from the second afternoon of practice when it occurred to him that the football thing was probably a kind of penance, and his first reaction was a certain amount of relief. Because before that he'd been wondering if he were actually developing a death wish, or at the very least a split personality. It was, he decided, related to guilt, all right. He wondered if breaking his leg would make him feel any less guilty. He doubted it. Probably the only thing that would help much would be breaking his neck.

As time passed, it became more and more obvious that guilt was what the whole thing boiled down to. There had been other emotions at first—shock and then pain and anger, but that passed over rather quickly. That was one thing Diane's betrayal had done for him. It had been painful but quick—like a kick in the mouth to cure a toothache. When he had found out what she had done, something had died; and in that dying he had been set free from the whole unrequited love syndrome. He didn't daydream about her anymore, or yearn for her or wonder if there was any way things could have turned out differently. Strangely enough, he didn't even hate her. The only person he hated was himself.

No, his guilt was because of the deer. It was knowing that on the first day of hunting season, the twenty-second of September, his stag would hear voices and come out confidently expecting apples and admiration and wait for the bullet that would leave him struggling on the green grass trying to breathe through his shattered lungs. And it would all be James Archer Fielding's fault. His fault even more than Diane's and her father's, because he had known the deer and understood what he signified, and they didn't and never could. He had known the deer and had traded away its life for something that, when you came right down to it, was not a whole lot different from what Diane and her father were after—a kind of trophy. Diane was to have been his twelve-pointer—his all-time-winning entry in the make-out record book for teenaged males.

So he really couldn't fault Diane for wanting the kind of trophy that counted in the world she'd been born into. But he could fault himself and he did, not only for the fate of the deer, but also for what he had done to Griffin and the two kids. He couldn't seem to stop seeing them in his mind's eye—Woody's rumpled, toothless face contorted in a howl of grief and rage, Griffin's dazed, wounded stare and, although he hadn't actually seen it, Laurel's funny, delicate face bloated and blemished by hours of crying.

When he wasn't thinking about all of that, about the misery he had caused and was causing and would cause in the future, he thought about his own stupidity. It was ironic, really. Here he was—a person who had always thought of himself as being somewhat more intelligent than the average, who finds that he has committed a terrible deed, not because of any evil intention but only through his own asinine, imbecilic, gullible, ridiculous, fat-headed stupidity. On top of everything else, it was terribly humiliating.

The humiliation of it all was probably the main reason he didn't tell anyone about it—not his parents, and certainly not Max. But when Charlotte asked about Diane, he admitted that she had been right.

"Oh, that's all over," he said. "You were right when you said we didn't have anything in common."

"Did I say that?" Charlotte asked. "I only remember asking you what you had in common."

"Okay, then. You would have been right if you *had*

said we didn't have anything in common."

"Well." Charlotte looked puzzled. "I can't help being a little bit surprised. She seemed so—well—enthusiastic, that day when she came to the cabin, just before we left."

He couldn't help wincing. She'd been enthusiastic, all right, but not about what he'd thought she was enthusiastic about. "I know," he said. "She acted that way sometimes. It didn't mean a whole lot."

"I see. Well, I must say, you don't seem to be terribly upset about the whole thing."

"About its being over? I'm not. That was another thing you were right about. About me getting over it. I did."

Charlotte smiled. "I'm quite overwhelmed. To have been right about you twice in rapid succession. I don't think I've done that well since you were six years old."

He returned her smile, but it wasn't easy because behind it he was thinking that she had been wrong about one thing—terribly wrong. She had been wrong to advise him to do something to get Diane back. Because he had done it, all right. He had really done it.

His mother looked at him closely. "Perhaps I should quit while I'm ahead, but I can't help making one more observation—about Diane. I have to admit she was quite —well—spectacular, and I can certainly understand your —ah—interest; but at the same time my general impression, and your father's, too, I might add, was not entirely favorable. I don't know if I can say exactly what it was. Something just didn't ring true."

He didn't say anything, and after a moment she went on. "Now, the other girl, on the other hand . . .

And don't take offense, because I'm not implying anything, I realize she is still quite a child. My feeling about her, that one time we met, was quite positive. There was a sensitivity . . ."

"Yeah," James said. "Look. I've got to get started, or I'll be late to class." There was plenty of time, actually. He just didn't want to hear about Griffin's sensitivity.

It was only a day or two after that conversation, on Wednesday of the last week before hunting season —the Wednesday of the last week of the deer's life—when the thing about Griffith Donahue was on the front pages of all the papers. Charlotte read it in the morning paper, and she told James about it as soon as he got home from school.

"They think she probably just ran away," she said, "but there is some concern that it might be a kidnapping. However, according to the papers there's been no demand for ransom. At least not yet."

James grabbed the paper.

Griffith Alexandra Donahue, thirteen-year-old daughter of the late Kevin Donahue and Alexandra Griffith Westmoreland, was reported missing last night by Mrs. Ardith Brownwell, headmistress of Honeywell School in Marin County.

Word of her daughter's mysterious disappearance again focuses public attention on Alexandra Westmoreland, heir to the vast Griffith fortune, whose childhood was marred by the prolonged and bitterly contested custody battles instigated by her estranged parents and her paternal grandmother. The object of constant media attention as a child, Mrs. Westmoreland remained in the public eye as a startlingly beautiful debutante, as a result of a succession of flamboyant and well publicized escapades, climaxed by her early elopement marriage to Kevin Donahue, daredevil mountain climber and race car driver. After her first marriage ended tragically in the fatal crash of Donahue's experimental racing car, Mrs. Westmoreland remarried and—

Near the end of the column James read something that clinched it, although he had been very nearly certain from the first moment.

According to Lt. Bryce, early fears of a kidnapping have been somewhat reduced by the discovery of a missing sleeping bag and by testimony given by Griffith's seven-year-old half-brother. The boy, Woodrow Everett Westmoreland III, has insisted that his sister told him she was going away, but that he does not know why, or what her destination might be.

Woody did know, though. James was sure of that. And he knew, too, beyond a shadow of a doubt.

That night James slept very little. Right at first, before he'd had time to think it all out, he very nearly told his parents. But thank God, he didn't. As sympathetic and understanding as they might be—and he felt fairly certain they would be, particularly his mother—they *were* parents. And as parents, their first thought would be about Griffin's parents, and how frightened and worried they would be. The first thing they'd do, James was certain, would be to insist that Griffin's parents be told—and that was exactly what he didn't want done—not under any circumstances.

He knew he might be sorry for his decision. If something terrible happened to Griffin—something that might have been prevented if her parents had been told—it would be all his fault. One more thing that would be all his fault.

And something might very easily happen to her. She had gone, of course, back to New Moon to try to save the deer; and there was no telling how she planned to go about it. There were only two or three ways James could think of, and all of them would be highly dangerous. She might try to lead the deer out of the box canyon to some other hiding place—or she could throw herself between the hunters and their prey like the Greenpeace protestors at the baby seal hunts. And those dangers weren't the only ones she might be facing. A thirteen-year-old girl alone in the Sierras could face any number of difficulties, including the possibility of being recognized and actually kidnapped.

Yes, it was certainly possible that any number of terrible things might happen to Griffin if he didn't tell; but to his way of thinking, none of them were worse than what had to happen if he did tell. If he told, Griffin's parents would be alerted that she was at New

Moon or on her way there, the police would be notified, she'd be picked up, the deer would die on September twenty-second, and Griffin would know who had betrayed her. She would know because the only others who might guess where she had gone were Woody and Laurel, and they would never give her away. So she would know that James had betrayed her a second time —except that he wasn't going to do it. It wasn't so much that he wouldn't do it, as that he couldn't. He didn't know why exactly, but it was simply something he absolutely could not do. And there was no one he could talk to about it—except possibly, Max.

It was after lying awake half of Wednesday night going over and over all the reasons why he ought to tell and the one simple unreasonable but completely unshakable reason why he couldn't and wasn't going to, James decided to discuss the matter with Max. Talking to Max was a possibility, because James knew that Max would never tell anyone else. Max had a very strict code of behavior, and one of the most important rules in it was that you never betrayed a confidence; or as Max was more apt to put it, you never ratted on a friend. Max often said he never ratted, and as far as James knew, he never did—except, of course, about sex. Max said that didn't count because nobody really expected you to keep quiet about sex any more. He had once, he said, because the girl had asked him to, and then he found out that she'd told half a dozen people in the next twenty-four hours, and half the school before the week was over. But on other matters, Max could be counted on to listen and keep his mouth shut.

The thing was, that while telling Max probably

wouldn't do anything to help Griffin, it might possibly keep James Fielding from going off his rocker completely. Not that it would matter a great deal if he did. In fact, there were times when he felt he really ought to be shut up someplace. Someplace where he couldn't wipe out anymore innocent animals and little kids. But on the other hand, if he did crack up, it might be hard on other innocent people—like his mother, for instance. So Thursday, on the way home from school, he told Max the whole story.

Max was a good audience. His face, a loosely related collection of features that often seemed to be engaged in several independent activities at once, seemed to consolidate as he listened. James knew he had Max's complete attention when a bunch of girls went by and he didn't even notice. But when James got to the part about what Diane had done, he interrupted to say that he knew the type.

"A Zelda," he said.

"A what?"

"A Zelda. Zelda Fitzgerald. F. Scott's wife. A girl whose motto is "Anybody who has so much deserves to have everything." I've been meat-axed by several of them. Not all beautiful girls are Zeldas, but enough of them are to make it an occupational hazard of fox hunting. It's something you have to learn to watch out for. Half the time when you get hold of a really gorgeous one, you suddenly notice that some vital part of your anatomy is missing."

"Yeah. Like your heart," James agreed ruefully.

"Or whatever," Max said. "Go on. What did you do then?"

So he went on—to the very end. He didn't leave anything out; and he thought he did a pretty good job of it, even the part about Griffin. It wasn't easy to put something as complicated and original as Griffin into words, but he felt he'd at least come close. When he finished, Max just looked at him for several seconds and then asked, "So what are you going to do about it?"

"I'm going to New Moon," James said.

"Yeah," Max said. "I thought that was what you were going to do."

CHAPTER 17

ALMOST immediately Max came up with a plan that would make it possible for James to leave the next morning—Friday—with no one having to know for almost four days. The first step was for Max to go home with James and tell Charlotte that his family was spending the weekend at a cottage on Bodega Bay and James was invited to go along. Charlotte was sure to say yes—she'd been telling James he was working too hard lately and needed to take a break. Their story would be that James would be going directly from school on Friday and would not be returning until Monday morning, so he should not be expected at home again until Monday after school.

Then on Monday afternoon, about the time his parents would be begining to worry, Max would deliver a note from James. The note would explain that he was away on very important business, the nature of which he couldn't disclose at the moment, and that they were not to worry because he was safe, in good spirits, not kidnapped, not running away, and would undoubtedly be home within a day or two.

"But what will you do if they insist on calling the police, in spite of the note?" James asked. "They'll probably grill you."

"I know," Max agreed. "Actually, I'm rather looking forward to it."

After the conversation with Charlotte, which went very smoothly, they went downtown to the after-hours window of James' bank and withdrew his life savings of twenty-seven dollars and thirty-three cents, and then to Max's house where James wrote the note for Monday, and where Max insisted on contributing what was left of his week's allowance, which he had been holding in reserve for a heavy date with Trudi Hepplewhite. It was a real sacrifice, and James appreciated it.

So the very next morning, after another almost sleepless night, James went down to breakfast, where he struggled with guilt and apprehension while his parents chatted about the nice, sunny weather and wondered if it would be warm enough to swim at Bodega Bay. By forcing himself, he managed to eat the proverbial hearty breakfast; and then, after saying good-by as casually as possible, he walked out the back door feeling as if he really were starting on that long last walk to a richly deserved doom.

He went first to Max's, where Max met him in the garage with a backpack. Max's whole family was into wilderness backpacking, and the set-up Max had prepared looked like enough for a whole family, and a large one at that. Max obviously expected James to be overwhelmed, and he was, especially when Max lifted it onto his shoulders.

"Wow," James said, struggling to keep from tipping over backward. "Are you sure you can spare all this stuff, Max?"

"Sure," Max said. "And don't worry about the weight. That pack is scientifically designed. After a while you won't even know it's there."

James said he was glad to hear that; and after thanking Max for everything, he said good-by and started out for the BART station. The plan was for him to go as far as he could by local transit since, according to Max, who had gone through a runaway phase at the age of nine, a long-distance ticket purchased near home is too easy to trace.

Traveling east during the westward commuter rush, he felt quite safe in the crowded station, but very conspicuous on the almost-empty eastbound car. He slumped in a corner seat, expecting at any moment to be accosted by any or all of five suspiciously innocent-looking fellow travelers—who would identify themselves as members of a special SWAT squad assigned to runaways and lead him off to jail. He left BART at the Concord station, and by catching local buses and hitchhiking, he made it as far as Sacramento by noon, and to the Greyhound bus station barely in time to catch the one-ten bus to South Tahoe. The bus ride was uneventful, and by five-thirty he had started the long hike from New Moon, around the perimeter of The Camp, to the Willowby property.

He kept to the woods at first, out of sight of Camp traffic, and when he was opposite the main gate he stopped to rest. Max's backpack, which obviously was scientifically designed for someone quite unlike James Archer Fielding, was already crushing his shoulders and turning his legs into strands of spaghetti. The gate was a temptation. If the guard on duty happened to remember him, he might let him in and out again at the west gate, which would cut miles off his journey. But he didn't dare risk being reported in a few days, when his name, as well as Griffin's might be in all the papers. So he gritted his teeth and trudged on around the outer fortifications of old T.J.'s stockade.

Beyond the gate, the road was deserted, and James walked in the middle of it—walked and slogged and staggered as the road climbed and dipped, curved and then curved back again. He began to stop and rest more and more often. The sun was setting, and he wanted very much to get at least as far as the Willowby property before setting up his camp for the night, but there were times when his feet simply refused to cooperate. Leaning against the trunks of trees, or sitting on fallen logs, he rubbed his aching shoulders, nibbled on the contents of a plastic envelope labeled Backpackers High Energy Mix, and watched the shadows darkening among the trees. And while he nibbled, he wondered what he thought he was doing out there all alone in the middle of nowhere. He also wondered if there was any chance at all that he would find Griffin, and if he did if he'd be able to help her. He even contemplated going home, once or twice. But each time he got up and went on again; and by the time it was really dark, he was so close to the Willowby cabin he decided to push on and spend the night there.

Actually there was very little reason to go on, since the cabin would be shuttered, locked and bolted, just as they had left it three weeks before. But each time he contemplated setting up his tent in the midst of endless open darkness, the urge to get to the cabin got stronger. So he dug a flashlight out of the backpack—of course there was a flashlight, he was lucky there wasn't a complete electric generator—and stumbled on down the narrow path of light. The cabin began to seem more and more like a refuge, a place of sanctuary that waited at the end of the ordeal, offering rest and comfort and safety. It must have been well after ten o'clock when he dragged himself up the stairs to the veranda, unrolled his sleeping bag against the wall, crawled into it and almost immediately fell asleep.

He woke in the morning to the familiar rusty creak of the old lounge swing. It was daylight, but just barely, and the sun was still only a halo of light behind the mountainous rim of the lake's deep bowl. He recognized the tangy essence of evergreen forest, but the crisp cool prophesy of approaching winter was new and different. Sniffing appreciatively, he began to feel, for the first time since leaving home, vaguely optimistic. There was a peacefulness in the calm, motionless air—but the swing was still creaking—in the breeze. He sat up quickly and looked behind him—and, of course, it wasn't there. He'd helped move it into the cabin himself, just before they left. As the faint rusty creak went on and on, he began to feel a crawling sensation on the back of his neck.

The sound seemed to be coming from the end of the veranda where the swing always sat, and as he crawled out of his sleeping bag and moved toward it, it got distinctly louder, but there was still nothing there. It wasn't until he was standing on the very spot that he realized the sound was coming from inside the house—

from just inside the shuttered window. Putting his ear to the crack in the heavy shutters he verified the fact. Just inside the window in the closed and shuttered room where he and William had put the swing, something was making it sway rhythmically back and forth. Listening to the slow, rusty squeak, James discovered that his heartbeat seemed not only to have magnified, but also to have proliferated so that it was thumping away not only in his chest, but also in his stomach, his throat and the roof of his mouth. Swallowing hard, he began to tiptoe backwards. When he reached the stairs, he reluctantly turned his back on the cabin and hurried down them.

Leaning against a tree several yards from the house, he began to think more rationally. Obviously, someone was in the house. Somewhere a door or a shuttered window had been forced and someone had gotten in. Moving cautiously, James began to reconnoiter.

When he had circled the entire cabin, he was more mystified than ever. All the doors were still locked and padlocked, and the windows were all shuttered, except for the small round one in the hall, which didn't open and was too small, anyway, to admit an intruder.

Tiptoeing back up the stairs, James went to the door and listened. The creaking had stopped. Raising his fist, he poised it for a firm, sharp rap, thought better of it, and was quietly gathering up his gear, when a voice from the foot of the stairs said, "What are *you* doing here?"

It was Griffin. It really was Griffin, dirty and touseled and dressed in torn jeans and a baggy old flannel shirt. Her face seemed thinner and her dark-fringed eyes more enormous, and she returned James' smile with a stare as warily distrustful as a trapped animal's.

"It's all right," he said. "I came to help you."

"To help me? How did you know I was here?"

"I read in the paper that you'd disappeared and I thought you'd probably come back here. To help the deer. So I decided to see if I could help you."

There was no thaw in the cold suspicious stare. "Did you tell anyone else?"

"No. Nobody."

She lowered her head and looked at him from shadowed eyes.

"Honestly. No one knows except my friend, Max, and he won't tell. He helped me set it up so no one will even know I'm gone until Monday." He briefly explained the scheme, and she listened intently; but when he finished, she was still distant and watchful. "Honestly, Griffin," he repeated. "I came to help. You and the deer."

She was nodding doubtfully when suddenly her eyes widened and she pointed at his backpack. "What's in there?"

"What isn't? Enough provisions for a full infantry battalion."

"Food?" she asked, and the way she swallowed as she said it told the story. A few moments later they were sitting on the top step of the veranda, and James was digging fruit and cheese and crackers and a variety of fancy survival mixes out of his pack. Griffin was eating as if she were starving. It turned out she very nearly was.

Between mouthfuls she told him how she'd left

school with only a sleeping bag stuffed into a large shopping bag, because a suitcase or backpack would have given her away. That had been on Tuesday; and that first day, before anyone knew she was missing, she'd dared to buy some food in bus stations and grocery stores; but after that she'd eaten very little until yesterday afternoon when she broke into the Willowby cabin.

"Broke in," James said. "How?"

"The little porthole window that doesn't have a shutter," she said.

"But it doesn't open."

"I know. I broke it and took out all the glass. And then I squeezed through. I had to do it because I was so hungry and I didn't dare go to The Camp or New Moon."

"But there wasn't much food in there, was there? I remember my mother saying Dr. Willowby didn't want us to leave anything that mice might get into."

"There were a few canned things. Peas and beans and one can of pineapple. Most of it's gone now. When you get back, will you tell Dr. Willowby that I'll pay for everything? The food and the window?"

She went on eating then, and James ate too. When they were finished, she thanked him for the food and smiled for the first time; but when he asked her about her plans, the curtain came down again. Her eyes went shallow and shielded and her voice tightened as she asked him why he wanted to know.

"Because I want to help. I want to save the deer. I want . . ."

But he could see she wasn't buying it. Wasn't believing a word he said. Was probably suspecting him of trying to find out what she was planning so he could report to the Jarretts. Grabbing her shoulders he shook her hard. "Goddamn it, Griffin. You've got to believe me: I didn't mean to betray the stag. You've got to listen to me."

She did listen then as he went through the whole stupid, sordid thing. All about how he'd fallen for Diane and how she'd used him and lied to him. But he didn't spare himself, either. He laid it all out—about how he kept on making excuses for her long after he should have been able to see what was happening, and how he convinced himself that if he could only get her attention away from the other guy for a little while, he'd be able to get her back. He explained how he hadn't really meant to tell her where the deer was, and how he had believed her promise never to tell. But even as he told it, he could see that there was no way he could make it understandable, because it wasn't. Even while he was telling it, he knew if he were Griffin he'd never forgive himself.

When he finished, she was staring at him with what looked like intense anger, and he shrugged hopelessly. At least he'd tried. He started to say, "I'm sorry," and found that they were saying the same thing—in unison. "You're sorry?" he asked. "What are you sorry for?"

"For blaming you. I don't anymore." She got to her feet. "I was just going back to the valley. Do you want to come? I'll show you my plan."

It took him a minute to shift mental and emotional gears. But it wasn't the first time that trying to account for Griffin's thought processes had made him feel like a computer with a few chips missing, so he recovered quickly and said great, that he couldn't wait to hear about her plan to save the deer. Of course, he was glad to hear that she had a plan, but he wasn't entirely confident that it would be workable, and he began to feel even more uneasy when he saw the pick-axe.

Just as he had feared, her plan was typically Griffin-esque—imaginative, courageous and not very realistic. She was planning to chop away the ledge at the highest point of the cliff trail so there would no longer be any access to the valley. The day before James arrival she'd actually begun work, chopping away at the rock ledge with Dan Willowby's enormous pickaxe.

"I got that much done yesterday," she said, pointing to a place where she'd managed to erode away an inch or two of the already dangerously narrow trail. "But it doesn't go very fast. See." She held out her hands, palm upwards, exposing rows of angry red blisters.

The shiver that slid down his spine could have been related to the blisters, or to the thought of swinging a pickaxe on that precarious perch. When she asked him if he thought it would work, he hesitated, and then put off saying what he really thought by suggesting that he'd think about it while they went to see the deer.

"I haven't seen him for a long time," he said. "Is he all right?"

"He's wonderful," Griffin said, and she put down the pickaxe and led the way on across the high trail.

Unlike the slopes around the lake, the sheltered valley was as yet untouched by the approach of winter. The meadow grass was still lushly green, jays screeched in the pines, dragonflies hummed over the creek bed, and the deer came out to meet them, quickly and confidently. Moving through the tall grass with a calm, measured dignity, he came to within a few yards of the boulder before he stopped. James could see the liquid sheen of his large eyes, the flare of his nostrils as he tested the air, and the small oval amulets that still dangled from his antlers, attached by ribbons, limp and faded now, but still faintly red.

James looked at Griffin. Sitting just as she had on that day in August when he had first brought her to see the deer, she hugged her knees against her chest and gazed with wide-fixed eyes—dreaming who-knew-what deer myths and stag legends. Dreams that, like the deer itself, were doomed to die in only two more days. Involuntarily he sighed sharply and heard Griffin's sigh echoing his. She turned to look at him, her eyes begging for reassurance."

"Do you think it will work?" she asked. "My plan?"

Feeling that to mention the plan's difficulties and dangers would only make her more determined he said, "Well, I don't know. I'm afraid the Jarretts won't give up that easily. If they can't get over the trail, they'll probably just go back and get mountain climbing equipment and try again. And besides, have you thought about what might happen to the deer if you make the trail impassable? He won't be able to get out either."

"I know. But couldn't he just go on living in the valley?"

"I'm not sure. I think he only stays there in the summer and fall."

She nodded. "Laurel said her uncle told about hearing rumors that skiers had seen a fantastic buck in this area during the winter, but no one ever saw it when the snow was gone. He said he'd always thought it was just a local legend—until Diane found out about the hidden valley."

"The thing is," James said, "he probably goes out every year at mating season and stays out during the winter."

"But it would be better for him to have to stay in the valley all the time than to be shot by the Jarretts," Griffin said. "At least he'd be alive."

"Well, maybe. I'm not sure there'd be enough food for him in this little valley in the wintertime. The snow must get very deep here. He might starve to death."

Griffin looked horror-stricken, and then completely crushed. "But what can we do?"

"I'm not sure," he said. "I'm thinking about it. We'll do something."

"But we only have until day after tomorrow," Griffin said.

"I know," he said. "But don't worry. We'll think of something."

CHAPTER 18

ALL the way back to the cabin they discussed what might be done to stop the Jarretts and save the deer's life. The possibilities were few. James mentioned his idea about trying to get the deer out of the valley, but Griffin said she'd thought of that, too, and had given it up. She pointed out that even if they were able to get him to leave the valley, he would still have the entire hunting season ahead of him, in an area crawling with other hunters as well as the Jarretts. As it became more and more evident that there was really nothing they could do, Griffin's suggestions became wilder and less practical—things like shooting at the Jarretts from a high point on the trail as they approached the valley. Not intending to hit anyone, she explained, but only to frighten them off. James' comment that the Jarretts would very likely shoot back—intending to hit someone—seemed to discourage her very little. When James asked if she had a gun, she said no, but couldn't he think of a way to get them one? It wasn't until he had firmly and repeatedly said he couldn't, that she reluctantly moved on to other possibilities.

By the time they neared the cabin, she was favoring what seemed like a desperate and hopeless last stand. They would go to the narrowest part of the cliff trail, sit down and refuse to move when the Jarretts appeared.

"They wouldn't be able to get past us, so they'd have to listen to us," she said. "And maybe we could make them understand why they shouldn't kill him."

It sounded like a very precarious version of a sit-down strike, and James didn't like the idea for several reasons.

"I doubt if they'd listen," he said.

"Well, then," she said almost casually but with an odd ring to her voice, "I'll tell them that if they don't promise not to kill him, I'll jump."

"Griffin." He grabbed her arm and turned her around to face him. She looked as if she actually meant it—calm, but with a light in her eyes that really scared him. He saw then the difference between Griffin's commitment and his own. He wanted to save the deer for reasons he could explain and others that he couldn't, and the ones he couldn't explain were probably the most significant. But even so, he knew there was a limit to his commitment—a point at which he would go no further. Griffin's reasons were undoubtedly all unexplainable, or at least it wouldn't occur to her to try; but her commitment was obviously frighteningly close to being unlimited.

"You can't do that," he told her. "I won't go with you; I won't even try to help anymore unless you promise me you won't do that."

She finally promised, but he wasn't entirely reassured. He would just have to come up with an alternate to the plan for a cliff trail confrontation.

By the time they reached the cabin, James was exhausted, feeling the need for a respite from desperate and hopeless strategies, for sleep, which he had had very little of for several nights, and in particular, for food. Preferably for food that hadn't been dehydrated, fortified and scientifically prepared for wilderness trail munching. When he mentioned the possibility of a hot meal, Griffin's troubled frown was replaced by one of her rare high-intensity smiles.

After she had wriggled her way back through the porthole window—a feat that James would never have thought possible—she unlatched the shutters on the kitchen windows, James climbed through, and lunch was underway. The temperamental stove responded to James' practiced coaxing, and before long they were sitting down to reconstituted pea soup, tuna and noodles and slightly stewed dried fruit. Griffin said she'd never tasted anything as good in her entire life.

With his stomach satisfied, rest and sleep moved into first priority. Three rather sleepless nights and yesterday's long strenuous hike were catching up with him. Watching Griffin bustling energetically around the sink, he sighed. As soon as she finished cleaning up the kitchen, she would undoubtedly want to get back to plotting and planning. Noticing the long wisps of hair that straggled free from her braid, the muddy smear on her chin and the decidedly grungy appearance of her plaid shirt, he was struck by a sudden inspiration—a scheme that might rechannel her energies long enough for him to get an hour or two of rest.

"How long has it been since you washed your hair?" he asked.

Griffin wiped her hand on her shirt and then reached up to smooth her hair and encounter a small twig that had become entangled in a stringy wisp. "Why?" she asked, looking at the twig.

"Well, it does seem to have collected a bit of debris. Doesn't it?" he asked. "If you want to make an impression on the Jarretts, if we see them . . ."

It worked. After firing up the stove again and helping Griffin find a collection of pots and pans and fill them with water, he was able to retire to his old room, stretch out on the bed, and collapse into a coma that must have lasted almost three hours. When he finally emerged, Griffin was sitting on the veranda railing drying her hair. She was wearing one of Dr. Willowby's enormous bulky knit sweaters, which hung down almost to her knees, and her skin had a freshly washed sheen. Various articles of wet clothing were draped along the railing beside her.

"I took a bath and washed some clothes, too," she said. "I feel a lot better."

"You look better," he said. "A lot better." She looked, in fact, surprisingly beautiful in an immature way, with her dark eyes and glowing skin and her long, thick curtain of light-streaked hair. She smiled uncertainly. "Did you have any new ideas?" she asked.

So they were back at it again. Back to plots and counterplots, hopes and fears, despair, brief hopefulness and despair again. It went on the rest of the afternoon, and by sunset they had only decided on a fall-back plan

—a last resort to be initiated if nothing better turned up.

According to the fall-back plan, they would go the next afternoon to the Jarretts' cabin. The Jarretts were sure to be there by then, making preparations for an early start the next morning on the first day of the season. Once there, they would simply go in and explain to the Jarretts why they must not shoot the deer. On the surface it seemed ridiculous, but James thought there was some hope. Perhaps not much hope that Hank Jarrett and his family might be moved when they saw Griffin and realized what she had risked in order to save the deer, but a very definite hope that Jarrett might be moved by realizing what the papers might make of the story if the deer were slaughtered. James intended to point out the negative publicity aspect of the situation very clearly. He would remind Jarrett of his previous run-ins with the Sierra Club and other conservation groups and what a new surge of bad press might do to his latest construction proposals.

When he had explained the bad press angle to Griffin, she agreed that it might work. She wasn't certain, but at least it was better than no plan at all; and afterwards she became calmer and more cheerful. On the top step of the veranda, curled up inside Dan's barrel-like sweater like a minnow in a lobster pot, she stared out over the lake in one of her strange trances. After a long time she sighed and said, "I have a feeling it might work, if I did everything right."

"What do you mean—if you did everything right?"

"The talismans. And the ceremony."

"Oh yes," he said. "Right. The talismans. Tell me about them. How are they supposed to work?"

Griffin uncurled herself and began to collect her washing. "It's getting cold," she said. "Let's go in and cook something."

But he decided not to let her get away with it that easily. "Look," he said, "if your magic can save the deer, why have you been so worried? Why have we been going to all this trouble?"

"Because—" She stopped and thought. "Because I don't know how it's going to work. It might work and the stag might get killed anyway—and that might be part of the magic, too. But I want it to work so that he doesn't die, so I have to go on doing everything I can. I think magic always works, but it doesn't always work just the way you think it ought to."

"Well, I hate to be critical, but that doesn't make much sense," James said.

"Doesn't it?" Griffin said. "No, I suppose it doesn't. But it doesn't really matter. Making sense doesn't have anything to do with making magic."

"That does it," James said. "How about macaroni and cheese and chili beans? Is that something that would make sense right now?"

"It sounds like magic," Griffin said.

After dinner they built a huge fire in the fireplace. Griffin took her sleeping bag off the swing and sat on it in front of the fire, and James pulled up Dan's old saggy-bottomed upholstered chair. Candle- and firelight made wavering shadows on the rough log walls and flickering reflections in the shuttered windows.

"I love this room," Griffin said. "It's like a bear's winter cave."

"Is that why you slept in here instead of one of the bedrooms?"

"Yes. The bedrooms frightened me. I like sleeping on the swing."

He told her then about how he'd heard the swing creaking that morning, and his rather violent reaction. They both laughed, and then she asked him to explain again about how he and Max had arranged it so his parents wouldn't know he was missing until Monday.

When he finished, she said, "I wish I could have done something like that. So my parents wouldn't have had to know."

She was leaning forward with her arms wrapped around her knees, staring into the fire, her face curtained by hair. But her voice had changed, as it always did when she mentioned her parents. It occurred to James that he had a perfect opportunity to test his theory about Griffin's emotional problems and how they stemmed from mistreatment and neglect by her jet-set mother. He knew, however, from past experience, that it wouldn't be easy to draw her out. There was probably just too much pain and anger involved. But it seemed like a good time to try. James Archer Fielding, psychiatrist. The doctor is in—minus a couch perhaps, but a sleeping bag in front of a roaring fire ought to do. He did a quick rerun of all the psychiatric type movies he'd seen and tried to recall a typical opening question. Preferably something disarming, but a little more to the point than, "Just say whatever comes into your mind, Miss Donahue."

After several minutes nothing very subtle had come

to mind, and he gave up and settled for a more forthright approach. "Tell me about your mother, Griffin."

Her head came up with a jerk, and she turned quickly to look at him.

"What about my mother?" she said.

Her frown startled him. "Nothing in particular. I'm just curious about her."

Her eyes searched his face.

"She just seems very interesting," he said. "And very beautiful."

She smiled uneasily.

"And she must lead a very fascinating life."

The frown returned. "She's had a very sad life," Griffin said. "Ever since she was born, she's had a very sad life."

James lost control of his face, and his eyebrows went up in surprise and disbelief.

The frown deepened. "The money doesn't help. It was the money that made it so awful, at least right at first. When she was just a baby and everyone wanted her for the money and pretended to love her and tried to make her hate all the others, only she always knew it was just the money they wanted, and none of them really loved her."

"Did she tell you that?"

"Yes. She's told me about it lots of times. And about how she always felt angry at them for only caring about the money, and that was why she did things to get even with them."

"Like what, for instance?"

"Well, like," Griffin began, but then she stopped suddenly and narrowed her eyes. "Like all the things everybody already knows about because it's all been in the papers and magazines."

"I don't know about it," James said. "My mother does, I guess. At least she said something about reading about your mother in the papers, but she didn't say much about what she read."

"Didn't she?" Griffin looked intrigued and then pleased. "I liked your mother."

"No, she didn't. So tell me. Like what?"

She shrugged. "Things like driving her stepfather's Rolls Royce into the ocean. And bringing a lot of people from a labor camp to her house for a party when her folks were away. And other things. The papers always told what she did, but they never told why she did things. And usually she had good reasons. Like when she ran away and married my father, the papers made it sound as if she only did it to get her name in the papers."

"Why did she really do it?"

"Because they were in love. She loved him more than anything in the world." Griffin's face had taken on the inward look it always had when she was involved in one of her fantasies—as if she had shut out the world and was tuning in on the data from some kind of internal tickertape. "They were very young and beautiful and happy," she said. "But then the car crashed and it was all over."

The therapy session was not moving in the direction he'd expected. Trying a different tack, he asked. "And how about your life? Has it been unhappy, too?"

"My life? No. My life is very happy."

"But isn't it pretty much like your mother's?"

"No. It's not like that at all. My mother needs me

and so does Woody, and I have friends and everything I want. Why do you think I'm not happy?"

"Oh, I don't know. I guess I just wondered about your parents. They seem to be very busy and gone a lot."

Griffin's dark eyebrows drew together, and her eyes blazed. "You be still. You just shut up about them. You're just like everybody else who gossips about her because she's beautiful and has money and interesting friends. They don't know what she's really like, and you don't either." Her eyes filled with tears, and she threw herself face down on the sleeping bag, burying her face in her arms and a tangled swirl of hair.

Well, so much for psychoanalysis, James thought ruefully. He'd read, of course, that it was a dangerous thing to fool around with if you didn't know what you were doing. But did he let that stop him? Of course not. Not Fielding, holder of the gold medal for the hundred yard dash with your foot in your mouth. So what if Mrs. Westmoreland didn't really deserve Griffin's loyal defense—would it really do Griffin any good right now to be forced to admit it. He slid down to the floor and touched her shoulder.

"Look," he said. "I'm sorry. I didn't mean to criticize your mother. Just like I said before, I don't know anything about her except that she's fantastically good-looking. I guess I just asked about her because I like you and I wanted to get to know you better. To understand about your life and things like that."

"Really?" Griffin's voice was muffled.

"Really."

There was another long silence, and James went

into the bathroom and got a washcloth; when he gave it to Griffin, she rolled over onto her back and put the cloth on her face. It was quite a while before she took it off, and when she did her long lashes were wetly dark as if she were wearing mascara. Her eyes looked, more than ever, like her mother's. She smiled faintly, and then just looked at James solemnly for such a long time he began to feel a little self-conscious. Finally her eyelids began to droop, and she went to sleep.

He must have gone on sitting there for quite a long time, alternately staring into the fire and watching Griffin sleep. Deeply relaxed, her hard young slenderness softened like a sleeping cat. The firelight made a smooth dome of her forehead and interesting shadows beneath her high cheekbones. A thick strand of hair looped her throat like a necklace and quivered rhythmically with the beat of her heart. He found himself thinking about what she would have to face when she woke up—confrontation with the Jarretts, and then the twenty-second of September.

As he drifted toward sleep himself, his thoughts and feelings began to get more and more complicated. It was all very incoherent and confusing, but most of it concerned Griffin's strange personality—a unique combination of wide-ranging enthusiasms, crazy dreams and ferocious loyalties. She really was an interesting kid.

CHAPTER 19

WHEN he woke up the next morning, back in his old Willowby bedroom, it took him a minute to remember where he was and why. Then it all came back. He'd flaked out on his old bed after Griffin had awakened and moved her sleeping bag to the lounge swing. Surprisingly, considering the day ahead, he seemed to have slept very well. Struggling out of Max's sleeping bag and into his clothes, he hurried from the room.

Griffin's sleeping bag was still on the swing, but she wasn't in it. She wasn't in the kitchen either, but the window was wide open, and when he stuck his head out and called, she answered from someplace nearby.

"Here I am. I'm coming," she called, and a few seconds later she climbed in the window. "I've been out on the veranda," she said, "watching the sky. It looks like there might be a storm coming."

She was wearing her jeans and shirt again, her hair was braided down her back, and she looked more like her old self. She smiled at James, but her face tensed as she asked, "Should we go right away? To see the Jarretts? Do you think they'll be here yet?"

"We might as well have some breakfast first," James said, "but then we can get started. It may take some time to find a way into The Camp. We'll have to get in without being seen. And by then the Jarretts may have arrived. If not, we can wait."

When breakfast was over and the cabin returned, as much as possible, to the condition in which they'd found it, they started out for The Camp. The sun, which had shone briefly, was hidden now by dark clouds, and a cold wind was rustling the pine trees.

"I suppose we have you to thank for this weather," he told Griffin.

"Me?"

"Sure. A storm this early in the year? It's obviously part of that hunter's whammy you concocted. There'll probably be a cloudburst tomorrow for the first day of the season."

They were walking single-file along the path to The Camp, and Griffin turned back to him, frowning. "If our plan works, we won't need a cloudburst. Do you think it's not going to work?"

"No," he said. "I think there's a very good chance it will work." There was no use worrying her by admitting how unsure he really was. But in reality, the more he thought about it, the more he feared that resting their case on an appeal to the Jarretts' compassion was going to be an exercise in futility. But it was their only hope, and he intended to go through with it.

They tried the fence first, following it for a long way looking for a place where a nearby tree or cliff might offer a way over the barbed-wire barricade that slanted outward from the top of the chain link fence. But the fence had apparently been constructed with such attempts in mind. After a long futile hike, they turned back towards the lake. A swim in the cold, choppy water was not inviting, but it was beginning to seem like the only possibility. But then, when they were passing the west gate, another long shot occurred to James. He would simply announce himself, using his old pass number. The chance that it would still be on the list at the main gate was slight, given T.J.'s passion for record-keeping, but it was worth a try.

When a familiar voice came over the speaker, "Main gate. Sergeant Smithers speaking. Who goes there?" James' heart sank. Smithers was the type who would go by the letter of the law—a law that would say that the Fieldings' passes had been cancelled at the end of August. But having gone this far James persevered.

"James Fielding. Pass number one, eight, five, four, six.

Silence.

"You remember me, Sergeant Smithers. The Willowby cabin."

"Willowby? Oh, yes. Fielding. You folks back for the hunting season?"

"That's right," James said truthfully.

"You been down to the office to renew your pass? I don't have any record of it."

"Well, actually, I'm on my way there now. You're not going to make me go all the way around to the main gate are you?"

There was another pause and then, "Well, I guess

not. You get down to the major's office right away, though, and get that pass renewed. Okay?"

James said okay, the buzzer sounded, and they were inside the fence.

They took the long way around, hiding at the sound of approaching cars and detouring through the woods as they passed each cabin, and it was past noon when they arrived at seventeen Gettysburg Avenue. The Jarretts were obviously already in residence. The blinds were up, the garage was open and Hank Jarrett's land cruiser was parked in front of the house. A surge of memories mingled with James' already considerable misgivings and exploded into a complete funk-out. To burst in on the Jarretts with Griffin in tow, to face Diane again for the first time since he'd found out what she'd done, knowing that she knew that he knew what she'd done—it was all just too much. He simply wasn't going to be able to make himself do it.

Grabbing Griffin's arm, he pulled her back among the trees. "Look," he said, "let's rest a minute and have something to eat and think about how we're going to do this." His throat felt tight, and he wondered if his voice sounded strange. He led the way to a log, sat down and began to dig through the backpack. "Here aren't you hungry? Have some survival mix."

So they sat down on the same log where he had sat so many times with Diane, and James tried to get granola down his dry throat while Griffin watched him so intently that he couldn't help wondering if she were reading his mind. Reading his mind and guessing how close he was to giving up on the whole thing.

"Look," he said finally. "I wonder if there's any

point in our doing this. I just don't think it's going to do any good."

She stared at him for only a moment and then got to her feet and started towards the drive. He caught up with her at the edge of the grove and grabbed her arm; and as she whirled to face him, he saw that her jaw was set and her eyes were full of tears. And then suddenly, he kissed her.

In a way it was as much of a surprise and shock to him as it must have been to her, because up until that moment he had still thought of her as a kid—or at least he thought he had. But it wasn't the kind of kiss you'd give a kid. Not that it was anything much, technically speaking. Compared to all the kissing drills he'd been through with Diane, this one was very brief and uncomplicated. But the way it hit him was what surprised him. The thing was, it happened without any intellectual or sexual promptings whatsoever—with only a sudden overwhelming need to do something about the look on Griffin's face. And it wasn't until he was doing it that he realized that he'd never in his whole life wanted anything so much or in so many different ways. And when it was over, and Griffin's face had gone from total misery to a kind of wondering welcome, he took her hand and started up the drive toward the Jarretts' cabin.

They were all in the kitchen. Diane and Mike and their father were sitting around the kitchen table, Mrs. Jarrett was standing near the breakfast bar, and Jacky was sitting on the floor in the corner. The kitchen table was covered with newspapers, and on the newspapers was what seemed to be a whole arsenal—guns and parts of guns, boxes of bullets and all kinds of gun-cleaning equipment. When James walked into the kitchen, they all looked very surprised; but when they saw Griffin they were obviously astounded.

James found himself strangely calm. The emotional upheaval he'd expected on seeing Diane didn't materialize. "We're here to talk to you about the deer," he said.

Jill Jarrett was the first one to get over her astonishment enough to say something. "Aren't you the Westmoreland girl?" she asked Griffin.

Griffin looked at her. "No," she said. "I'm Griffith Donahue." Then she turned to the others. "We've come to ask you not to shoot the deer," she said.

"Do you know the police are looking for this girl all over the country?" Mrs. Jarrett asked James.

"Yes," James said. "I know." Jill Jarrett's face was absolutely rigid with curiosity. Her husband was frowning. Mike seemed to be vaguely amused, and Diane— Diane was still sitting at the table, clutching a rifle in both hands and staring at James with an expression that definitely looked like outraged anger. As if he had been the one who had somehow betrayed her.

"Look, Mr. Jarrett," he said. "Could we go someplace and talk for a few minutes. I'd like to talk to you alone."

Hank Jarrett stood up, wiped his hands on an oily rag and said, "Well, that just might be a good idea, young man. It looks to me like you've got a lot of explaining to do to someone; and since this young lady's parents aren't around, you might as well start with me." Then he led the way down the stairs to the trophy room.

Alone with Jarrett, it went better than James had expected. He told the whole thing briefly, starting with his own discovery of the valley and the deer and how he happened to share the secret with Griffin and her brother and Laurel. Laurel Jarrett, Mr. Jarrett's own niece, who loved the deer almost more than anyone else did. James stressed that point carefully, and he also remembered to stress the certainty of full media coverage of the whole story. The entire country would want to know all about why Griffin ran away and what the deer had meant to her and how she had tamed it, and how she would feel if it were killed.

Jarrett really seemed to be listening. He only interrupted once or twice to ask questions, and one other time when Jacky came downstairs and stood in front of them staring at James and swinging the hand that held the golf ball back and forth. James was definitely loosing his train of thought when Jarrett interrupted and sent Jacky back upstairs.

James finished his story, feeling that he'd made some headway; and after Jarrett started talking, he still thought so—for a while. Hank Jarrett began by saying that he understood how Griffin and Laurel felt about the deer, and that if it was up to him he might be willing to let the old buck live, even though he probably wouldn't have too many more years anyway, and very likely no more years at all in this particular condition, since a buck past his prime tended to produce less and less perfect antlers.

"In another year or two, he'll be of no use to anyone," Jarrett said. "Too tough to make good venison and with a deformed and asymmetrical rack, whereas at the moment he represents a trophy that would break just about every existing record."

James was trying to think of a polite way to point out that not everybody shared his enthusiasm for that kind of broken record, when Jarrett went on. "However, as I said, if it was just up to me, I'd say okay, let's let the old buck die a natural death since that's what the kiddies want; but the thing it, I have a kiddie of my own to think about. Diane wants this trophy very badly, and I've more or less promised it to her; and young as she is, I feel she's really earned it. She's worked hard at her marksmanship for years and especially all this last month. And, like I told you before, she's a natural with firearms. Almost never makes a bad shot, so at least you wouldn't have to worry about her messing up and making the buck suffer more than necessary. I kind of feel she deserves this one, so before I take this opportunity away from her, I'm going to have to get her okay on it."

James' heart sank. Leaving it up to Diane would have sunk it anyway, but remembering the expression on her face a few minutes before, it really hit bottom. He had a very strong feeling that if Mr. Jarrett was going to let Diane decide the deer's fate, there was almost no hope at all.

Back in the kitchen Mike was filling a glass at the sink, but everyone else was pretty much where they had been before. Diane was still working on a rifle at the table, and Griffin was standing near the door with her back to the wall, looking pale but determined. Behind her, torrents of windblown rain were slanting across the window. The storm had obviously arrived.

"Di, baby," Hank Jarrett said, "this young man has a very big favor to ask of you. I want you to listen to what he has to say, and then it will all be up to you. I've told him it has to be your decision."

Diane turned her chair around, but she went on fooling with the gun as James talked. The tension in the room was so high you could almost hear it, like a crackle of electricity. James had trouble with his voice at first, but it settled down and he began to tell it all over again, just about the same way he'd told it to her father. When he got to the part about taking Griffin to see the deer, Diane's eyes flickered up at him and her lip curled. "So it wasn't such a big secret after all," she said.

There was a silence broken only by the increasing whine of the wind and the drumming of rain on the window. "It was still a secret after Griffin and the kids knew," James said. He wanted to say it wasn't they who lied about keeping it a secret, but he knew there was no use antagonizing her anymore than necessary, so he just went on to tell why Griffin had run away—and how he had guessed, and followed her.

When he stopped, no one said anything for a long time. Everyone was looking at Diane; but she only went on looking down at the gun. She seemed to be breathing hard.

"Di," her father said, "what do you think? There is your little cousin to consider, you know. And this thing about the newspapers. Some of those conservation crackpots who made such a fuss about The Camp are going to have a real field day over this one."

"Daddy!" It was almost a scream. Diane jumped to her feet and started toward her father. The gun was still in her hand, and it crossed James' mind that she shouldn't be handling a gun when she was so emotionally upset. But at least she was remembering to carry it correctly, with the barrel pointed towards the floor. Running to her father, she grabbed the front of his jacket. "Daddy," she said again, stamping her foot, "you promised me. You said I'd earned it. You promised."

Hank Jarrett put his arms around Diane. "Now, now, baby. It's all right. I know I did promise. You know I don't go back on my promises."

It seemed as if it was all over, and Diane had won. James turned to Griffin, to take her away and try to comfort her, but at that moment someone yelled, "No! Jacky. No!"

James put his hands over the back of his head and ducked; the golf ball whistled past him, and the whole kitchen seemed to explode in a deafening roar. For just a second he thought it was thunder, but of course it wasn't.

CHAPTER 20

IT WAS an unusually fat letter, and James took it to his room to open it. Sitting on his bed, he tore off the flap and took out several newspaper clippings and a short letter written on notebook paper.

One of the clippings was from a Sacramento paper. It was about the recent return of Henry Jarrett, prominent local contractor, after a hospital stay in South Tahoe. Jarrett, the paper said, had been admitted to the hospital in late September following a hunting accident, which had occurred when his fifteen-year-old daughter, Diane Jarrett, had been struck by a golf ball, causing her to accidentally discharge the high-powered rifle she was carrying at the time. According to the article, the bullet, after having passed through her father's left foot and a hardwood floor, struck a valuable hunting trophy in the room below. Apparently the trophy, the stuffed head of an Alaskan moose, had been permanently damaged, but Jarrett it seemed, would eventually be almost as good as new.

The article didn't offer any explanation of the rather peculiar fact that Diane Jarrett had been struck by a golf ball while she was standing in the middle of her own kitchen. Jacky wasn't implicated. For that matter, neither were James and Griffin. Griffin hadn't been mentioned in any of the articles about the Jarrett accident, and James hadn't been mentioned in any articles at all. In spite of the fact that he'd gone to considerable lengths to see that it turned out that way, there were times when he couldn't help feeling a little left out.

The other articles were all about Griffin's disappearance and subsequent reappearance at her parents' summer home near the village of New Moon in the Sierra Mountains. As far as the public knew, she had gotten there entirely on her own and for reasons that were entirely her own. It hadn't been too difficult to arrange.

Griffin's letter, written in her now-familiar curly backhand on the back of what seemed to be an aborted English assignment, mostly concerned the future. In his last letter, James had said something about the stag's temporary safety; and apparently Griffin thought he had implied that the Jarretts' would go after him again next year.

"I don't think they will," her letter said. "I told Diane about the talismans while you were downstairs talking to her father. She didn't believe me then, but I think she does now. And besides, I don't think they'll want something around to remind them of what happened—not even a record-breaking trophy."

She just might be right about that. He certainly hoped so. Hoped the deer was safe. There had been no mention of it in the papers, so no one else would know. And Mr. Jarrett himself had said that probably the deer would be valueless as a trophy after this year. So there was reason to be optimistic.

The rest of the letter was about next summer. Griffin wanted to know if his parents had decided yet about renting the Willowby cabin again. In his next letter he would make it clear that he was definitely planning to be in the New Moon area whether his parents rented the cabin or not. He could always get a job in New Moon.

There was still a bulge in the middle of the envelope—a bulge that turned out to be a small flat oval of soapstone with a hole drilled in one end and an overall pattern of strange hieroglyphics. One of Griffin's talismans.

Collapsed on the bed with the talisman in the palm of his hand, he lay for a long time with his mind freewheeling. Suddenly, for the first time in months he began to feel a poem coming on. The first few lines wrote themselves. "To give tomorrow to a king | Tie it with ribbons to his crown | A talisman's a future thing . . ."

What came next was going to take some careful thought.